The Red Ribbon

LUCY ADLINGTON

CANDLEWICK PRESS

Copyright © 2017 by Lucy Adlington

First U.S. edition 2018

Library of Congress Catalog Card Number pending
ISBN 978-1-5362-0104-8

18 19 20 21 22 23 LSC 10 9 8 7 6 5 4 3 2 1

Printed in Crawfordsville, IN, U.S.A.

This book was typeset in Berling.

Candlewick Press
99 Dover Street
Somerville, Massachusetts 02144

visit us at www.candlewick.com

In memory of my grandmother, born E. R. Wild,
and in tribute to the original Betty

"Life is our cry. We have kept the faith!" we said;
"We shall go down with unreluctant tread
Rose-crowned into the darkness!"
—Rupert Brooke, "The Hill"

Green

It was really hard to run in such stupid shoes. The mud was thick as molasses. The woman behind me had the same problem. One of her shoes got stuck. That slowed her down. Good. I wanted to arrive first.

Which building was it? There? No—here. This one. I stopped dead. The woman behind nearly ran slap-bang into me. We both looked at the building. It had to be the right place. Should we just knock now? Were we too late?

Please let me not be too late.

I stood on tiptoe and peered through a small, high window at the side of the door. I couldn't see much, mostly my own reflection. I pinched my cheeks to get a bit of color and wished I had a dab of lipstick. At least the swelling around my eye had just about gone down, although the greeny-yellow bruise was still there. I could see straight; that was the main thing. Thick waves of hair would've hidden the rest. But . . . you make the best of what you've got.

"Are we too late?" the other woman wheezed. "I lost one of my shoes in the mud."

When I knocked at the door, it opened almost immediately, making both of us jump.

"You're late," snapped the young woman in the doorway. She looked us up and down with hard eyes. I looked back. Three weeks away from home and I still hadn't learned to grovel properly, no matter how much I got hit. This bossy girl—not much older than me, really—was all angles, with a nose so sharp it could've cut cheese. I've always liked cheese. The crumbly sort you have in salads, or the creamy cheese that's nice with fresh bread, or that really strong stuff with green fur that old people like on crackers . . .

"Don't just stand there!" razor-face scowled. "Get inside! Wipe your shoes! Don't touch anything!"

In we went. I'd made it. I was at the grandly titled Upper Tailoring Studio, otherwise known as a sewing workshop. My idea of heaven. The moment I heard there was a job here, I knew I had to get it.

Inside the workshop I counted about twenty heads bent over whirring machines, like fairy-tale characters caught in a spell. They were all clean; I noticed that straightaway. They were wearing plain brown overalls—nicer than the sack-thing slipping off my shoulders, that was for sure. Wooden tables were scrubbed bone white and covered with patterns and threads. In one corner were shelves of fabrics, showing so much unexpected color I had to blink. In another corner there was a cluster of headless, limbless dressmaker mannequins. I heard the hiss and clunk of a heavy iron and saw specks of lint floating by like lazy insects.

No one looked up from their work. They were all sewing as if their lives depended on it.

"Scissors!" came a cry from nearby. The worker at the nearest machine didn't even pause. Her foot kept working the treadle, and she eased the fabric under the needle even as she picked up the scissors. I watched them get passed along the table, hand to hand, then *snip*, set to a length of forest-green tweed.

The sharp girl who'd opened the door snapped her fingers in my face.

"Pay attention! I'm Marta. I'm in charge here. *The boss*—understand?"

I nodded. The woman who'd come in with me just blinked and shuffled her one-shoe feet. She was pretty old—about twenty-five—and as twitchy as a rabbit. Rabbits make good gloves. I had slippers lined with rabbit fur once. They were really cozy. I didn't know what had happened to the rabbit. I suppose it went in a stew . . .

Time to focus.

"Listen carefully," Marta ordered. "I won't say all this again, and—"

Bam! The door opened once more. The spring breeze blew another girl inside, one with hunched shoulders and round cheeks, like a squirrel that's just dug up a hoard of nuts.

"So sorry."

The new arrival gave a shy smile and looked at her shoes. I looked at them too. One was a sickly green satin slipper with a metal buckle, the other a leather brogue with broken laces.

We'd all been tossed random shoes when we were first given clothes here, but hadn't this little squirrel even managed to bargain a proper pair? I could tell straightaway she was going to be useless. Her accent was awfully, awfully . . . *you know*. Posh.

"I'm late," she said.

"No kidding," Marta replied. "Seems we've got quite a *lady* in our midst. How very kind of you to join us today, *madam*. How can I be of service?"

"They said there was a sudden vacancy at the Tailoring Studio," Squirrel replied. "That you needed good workers."

"Damn right I do! Real dressmakers, not *la-di-dah* ladies. You look like the sort of princess who's sat around on a cushion embroidering lavender bags and other useless frivolities. Am I right?"

Squirrel didn't seem offended no matter how much Marta sneered. "I can embroider," she said.

"You'll do what I order!" replied Marta. "Number?"

Squirrel put her feet together nicely. How did she manage to look so poised in that mismatched footwear? She was *not* the sort of girl I'd normally mix with. Even though she was dressed so badly, she probably thought I was too common. Beneath her.

She recited her number with perfect enunciation. Here it was all numbers, not names. Me and Rabbit reeled off our numbers too. Rabbit stuttered a bit.

Marta sniffed. "You!" She pointed to Rabbit. "What can you do?"

Rabbit-woman shivered. "I . . . I sew."

"Idiot! Of course you do, or you wouldn't be here. I didn't put out a call for seamstresses who can't sew. This isn't some excuse to slack off from doing tougher jobs! Are you any good?"

"I . . . I sewed at home. My children's clothes." Her face crumpled like a used handkerchief.

"Oh god, you're not going to cry, are you? I can't stand snivelers. What about *you?*" Marta turned to glare at me. I shriveled up like chiffon under a too-hot iron. "Are you even old enough to be here?" she scoffed.

"*Sixteen,*" said Squirrel suddenly. "She's sixteen. She said so before."

"I wasn't asking you, I was asking *her.*"

I swallowed. Sixteen was the magic number. Any younger, and you were useless.

"She's, er, right. I'm sixteen."

Well, I would be. Eventually.

Marta snorted. "And let me guess—you sew dresses for dollies and can just about stitch a button on, once you've finished your homework. Honestly! Why do they waste my time with these cretins? I don't need schoolgirls. *Get out!*"

"No, wait, you can use me. I'm a, um—"

"You're a what? A mama's girl? A teacher's pet? A waste of space?" Marta started walking away, with a little dismissive flip of her fingers.

Was that it? My first real job interview—failed. That meant going back to a job as kitchen maid or laundry scrubber at best. At worst, quarry work or . . . or no work at all, which was the worst thing that could happen.

My grandma, who has a motto for every occasion, always says, *When in doubt, chin up, shoulders back, and be bold.* So I straightened to my full height, which was pretty tall, took a deep breath, and declared, "I'm a cutter!"

Marta looked back at me. "You? A cutter?"

A cutter was a super-skilled sewer responsible for creating the shapes that would turn into actual clothes. No amount of decent dressmaking could save a garment botched by a bad cutter. A *good* cutter was worth her weight in gold. I didn't need gold. I just needed this job, whatever it took. It was my dream job — if you could have dreams in a place like this.

Up to that point the other workers had ignored us. Now I sensed they'd been listening in all along. Without missing a stitch, they were waiting to see what would happen next.

"Yes," I continued. "I'm a trained pattern-drafter, cutter, and tailor. I . . . I do my own designs. One day I'll have my own dress salon."

"Ha! That's a joke," Marta sneered.

The woman on the nearest machine spoke without even taking the pins from her mouth. "We need a good cutter, since Rhoda got sick and left," she murmured.

Marta nodded slowly. "That's true enough. All right. Here's what's going to happen. You, Princess, can take over doing ironing and scrubbing. Those soft hands of yours need toughening up."

"I'm not a princess," said Squirrel.

"Move!"

Marta looked me and Rabbit up and down.

"As for you two pathetic excuses for seamstresses, you can have a trial. I'll be blunt: there's only room for one of you. *Only one*, do you understand? And I'll chuck you both out if you fail to meet my high standards. *I* trained in all the very best places."

"I won't let you down," I said.

Marta seized something from a nearby pile of clothes and tossed it to Rabbit. It was a linen blouse, dyed such a fresh shade of mint you could practically taste it.

Marta gave her orders. "Rip the seams and let it out. It's for a client—an officer's wife—who drinks her cream by the jugful, so she's rounder than she thinks she is."

Cream . . . oh, cream! Poured over strawberries from my grandma's best green-flowered jug . . .

I caught a glimpse of the label inside the blouse collar. My heart almost stopped beating. It was the elegantly scrolled name of one of the most revered couture houses in the world. The sort of place where I wouldn't dare even to stare in the windows.

"And *you*"—Marta slapped a piece of paper into my palm—"another client, Carla, has asked for a dress.

Semiformal, for a music concert or something this weekend. Here are her measurements. Memorize them — I want the paper back. You can use the number four mannequin. Get fabric from over there."

"What?"

"Choose something to suit a blonde. Scrub yourself first at that sink and put overalls on. In this workshop, cleanliness is essential. No grubby finger marks on the fabric, no bloodstains or dust. Understand?"

I nodded, desperate not to start crying.

Marta's thin lip curled. "You think *I'm* severe?" She narrowed her eyes at me and jerked her head to the far end of the room. "Just remember who's standing in the corner."

At the back of the workshop there was a dark figure propped against the wall, picking at her cuticles. I glanced once, then looked away.

"Well?" said Marta. "What are you waiting for? The first fitting's at four."

"You want me to make a dress from scratch, before four? That's—"

"Too hard? Too soon?" she jeered.

"That's fine. I can do it."

"Go on then, schoolgirl. And remember, I'm expecting you to botch up, big time."

"I'm Ella," I told her.

I don't care, said her blank expression.

* * *

The workroom sink was one of those massive ceramic things, with green streaks under the taps where the pipes had wept. The soap barely lathered, but it was better than nothing — which was all I'd had for the past three weeks. There was even a towel — *a towel!* — for drying hands. Seeing clean water coming out of a tap was mesmerizing.

Squirrel, right behind me waiting her turn, said, "Looks like liquid silver, doesn't it?"

"Shh!" I frowned, conscious of the shadow of that dark figure at the far end of the room.

I took my time washing. Squirrel could wait. Even if I wasn't posh like her, I knew how important it was to be clean and well presented. Appearances matter. When I was a kid Grandma always made a *tsk-tsk* noise if I came in with grubby hands and dirty nails, or a suspicion of grime in hidden corners. *You could grow potatoes behind your ears!* she'd say, if I hadn't done a thorough rub with the washcloth.

Clean hands mean clean work was another of her mottoes. She also liked muttering *Waste not, want not*. And if anything mildly bad happened, she'd shrug and say *Better than a smack in the eye with a wet kipper!*

I never much cared for eating kippers, not when the house stank of fish for days afterward, and there were always bones, even when Grandma said, *Don't worry, it's boneless.* So you'd start in on the flesh, and then you'd gag as one of those spindly bones pronged the back of your throat. You'd have to hold up your napkin to root it out without revolting everyone else at the table. You'd put it on the side of your plate and try not to look at it for the rest of the meal. But you'd know it was there.

Since coming to Birchwood I'd already decided I was only going to see things I wanted to. Every second of my first three weeks had been horrible—things far worse than kipper bones. I'd been like a golem—a girl without a soul—shoved this way and that, waiting, standing, squatting. Now, in the sewing workshop, I suddenly felt human again. If I truly narrowed my mind, I could believe that nothing in the world existed except making this dress for my client, Carla.

A fitting at four. It just wasn't possible. Not designing, cutting, pinning, tacking, sewing, pressing, and finishing. I was going to botch it, just as Marta had said. I was going to fail.

Don't think failure, my grandma would say. *You can do anything you set your mind to. Anything. Except bake. You make lousy cakes.*

As I stood there, close to panic, I felt eyes on me. It was Squirrel, over at the ironing board. She was probably laughing at me. Why wouldn't she?

I turned my back on her and went *clomp-clomp* in my stupid too-big shoes to the shelves of fabric . . . and promptly forgot all about Marta and her threats. It was just so wonderful to see colors that weren't *brown*: three weeks of nothing but wood-brown, mud-brown, and other browns too horrible to mention.

Now there were rivers of material for my fingers to wade into. Marta had said this Carla was blond. Out of Birchwood's brown, green grew in my mind: a good color for blondes. I tugged at folds and bales of fabric, searching for the perfect shade. There was moss-green velvet. Silver-spangled gauze the shade of grass in moonlight. Crisp cottons with leaf prints. Satin ribbons ripe with light . . . And my favorite — an emerald silk that rippled like cool water under dappling trees.

Already I could see the dress I would make. My hands began sketching shapes in the air, fingertips touching invisible shoulders, seams, and skirt gores. I looked around. I needed things. A table and paper. A pencil, pins, scissors, needle, thread, sewing machine, BREAKFAST.

"Excuse me." I tugged on the sleeve of a sapling-thin girl swaying past. "Can you tell me where to get —"

"Shh," the girl said. She put two fingers to her lips and mimed a zip fastening them shut. She had ridiculously elegant hands, like a nail-polish ad but without the polish.

I opened my mouth to ask why talking was forbidden, then thought better of it. The dark figure in the corner didn't appear to be watching or even listening, but you never knew.

The thin girl — Giraffe, I labeled her — signed for me to follow her along rows of workers to the far end of a trestle table. She pointed to an empty stool. Three women were already sitting there. They hunched up to make room for me. One of them was Rabbit, nervously pulling the mint-green blouse inside out and peering at the seams.

13

I sat down with my silk. Now I needed to make a pattern. A girl farther down the table had a roll of pattern paper and a stubby pencil. I took a deep breath. Got up. Mimed that I wanted the paper. The girl bristled, just like a hedgehog. She pulled the paper closer. I put my hand on the roll and pulled it hard. Hedgehog tugged. I tugged back. I won. I took her pencil, too.

Marta was watching. Did I imagine she smiled? She gave a little nod, as if to say, *Yes, that's how it works here.*

I rolled the paper out. It was plain brown, shiny on one side and faintly striped on the other. The sort of paper we used to wrap sausages in. Lovely plump sausages with bits of chopped onion, or sometimes tomato sausages, violently red in the frying pan. Or herb sausages flecked with green basil and thyme . . .

My stomach growled.

Grandma always used newspaper for patterns. She could sketch out a complete dress or suit pattern in seconds, straight onto the pages of the local gazette. Then she'd snip through the headlines, the ads for medicinal tonics and the racing results. You never needed more than one fitting with Grandma's patterns. Me, I had to squint a bit first and do a few faint trial runs. Usually I had Grandma looking over my shoulder when I cut. Now I was on my own. I could hear a clock in my head ticking. First fitting at four . . .

Right. The pattern was drawn.

"Hey," whispered one of the hunched women opposite.

14

She was wide and squat with blobby skin, like a frog. "Save me any scraps of paper, will you?" she asked.

Frog was doing buttonholes on an apple-green wool coat. It was the sort of coat that's just right for spring if you can't decide whether it'll be warm or cool. We used to have an apple tree in the front yard of our house. It always seemed like *forever* before the blossoms became buds. One year the branches were loaded with fat fruit, and bent just like my back as I sewed. We had apple crumble flecked with caramelized sugar, flaky pastry apple turnovers, and even apple cider, which made me hiccup from the bubbles. When the War started, one of our neighbors chopped the tree down for firewood. They said Our Sort didn't need trees.

"The *paper?*" Frog broke into my thoughts.

I glanced around. Was saving paper scraps allowed? Before I knew how to reply, Frog had made a face at me and turned away.

I swallowed and called, "Scissors!" in a croaky voice. And then louder: "Scissors!"

Just like I'd seen before, a sharp pair of fabric shears was handed — slowly — along the tables. They were a decent set of steel scissors with double-sided handles. Grandma would have approved.

I swallowed again. "Pins?"

I'd already caught sight of Marta's pin tin, tucked in a pocket of her overalls. She came over. Counted out twenty. I told her I'd need more.

"My grandma says it's best to put them head to tail on silk so it stays in place."

"You're making the dress up in *silk?*" Marta said it like I'd signed my own death sentence. "Don't wreck it!"

She sniffed and moved off. I envied her. She had a roomful of people twitching to follow her orders. Plus decent shoes, a nice-ish dress under her overalls, and *lipstick*. She was a prominent. Prominents had privileges and power—just enough power to rule over the rest of us. Some prominents tried to be fair. Most loved being bullies, just like those kids at school who thought squashing others made them bigger and better. Out in the wild, if Marta was an animal, she'd be a shark, and we'd all be little fish in her ocean.

Little fish get eaten. Sharks survive.

The pins weren't the right sort. Not the tiny "li'l" pins that Grandma taught me to use for silk, so in the end I didn't dare put too many in, in case they left holes. The scissors terrified me too. Usually I love the sound of scissors cutting, and the flutter of excitement that goes with it. This time I felt pure fear. Once fabric is cut, it can't be uncut. You have to be so sure where you want those flashing blades to slice the weave.

I put my hands flat on the table until they stopped shaking. I was standing to do the cutting, but my legs felt weak. Grandma liked to do her cutting on the floor, where there was more room. I wasn't convinced the floorboards in the sewing workshop were clean enough for that. Instead I spread the silk on the table, pinned the paper, marked on darts and tucks . . . and prepared to do the deed.

When you start cutting, use the middle of the blades of your scissors and cut with long, even strokes. If only it was that easy. Today the fabric slithered like a snake in a meadow, winding between weeds looking for a mouse to eat. There were no mice in the workroom — no crumbs for them. No food for us either. Just air and lint and a touch of dust.

Rabbit eyed my scissors. Stealthily her hands crept across the workbench toward them. I snatched them up and began snipping at imaginary loose threads. Rabbit swallowed and whispered, "Please may I . . . ?"

I pretended not to hear her. I don't know why. When I couldn't stall any longer, I passed the scissors over.

"Thank you," she mouthed, like I was the spirit of selflessness.

It made me cringe to see her snipping clumsily away at that couture blouse. It had a white lace collar over the green, like cow parsley flowers in a hedgerow.

I guessed it was afternoon by the time I'd finished cutting and piecing together the dress. There's no lunch in Birchwood, so nothing to signal midday. When I'd been working outdoors I only knew it was noon when the sun was at its highest and hottest. That was the halfway point between breakfast and supper. In the clockless sewing room, time was marked by the clank of scissors set down on wood, the sigh of needle-pulled thread, and the tireless *whirr* of

17

the machines. Every so often there'd be a tinkle of metal falling to the floor, and Marta would call, "Pin!" Behind her back the other workers rolled their eyes and mocked her in a silent, rippling echo of *Pin! Pin! Pin!*

The dark figure at the far end of the room barely moved. I think she must have fallen asleep.

Suddenly Marta was at my shoulder. "Done yet, schoolgirl?"

"It's all tacked and ready to sew," I said.

Marta pointed me toward a sewing machine. My hands trembled as I set up the spool and threaded the needle. *First fitting at four . . .*

I pressed my foot to the treadle, ready to set it all in motion. The needle bobbed up and down — too fast! The thread snarled. Blood rushed to my cheeks. But no harm done — yet.

I tried again. Better. I checked the thread tension, made a few adjustments, took a deep breath, and began.

It was a familiar sound — the chatter of the metal parts all moving together. Part of me felt whisked away to Grandma's sewing room back home. I used to play on the floor while Grandma did her dressmaking, picking up pins and pieces of snipped thread. Grandma called her sewing machine Betty. Betty was old. Quite a work of art. It was decorated in black enamel with gold patterning and Grandma's name etched onto it. Grandma worked the treadle in her favorite moleskin slippers, cut at the front so her swollen feet could bulge out. When she sewed, the fabric seemed to guide itself in a straight line to the needle. I didn't yet have that magic touch. Or Grandma hovering over me to help.

A tear did fall then. It turned the silk a dark, poisonous green. I sniffed. No hankie. This was not a good time for memories. Better just to sew, one seam, one dart at a time. First the bodice pieces, then the skirt pieces, sleeves, and shoulder pads.

After each seam I leaped up from the machine and went to Squirrel at the ironing board. Frequent pressing is the secret to a neat garment — even a beginner knows that. The workshop iron had a long cord dangling from the ceiling. I prayed the iron wouldn't scorch or pucker the silk, especially since Squirrel-girl didn't seem to know quite what she was doing with it. She'd probably never done housework in her life.

Haven't you ever ironed before? I mouthed the first time I went up there.

Squirrel gave a rueful smile and shook her head. She mouthed: *The iron's heavy. And hot.*

I mouthed back fake surprise: *Who'd've thought?!*

Squirrel held out her hands for my silk. She spat on the iron to see how hot it was. The spit sizzled. She turned the thermostat down. When she actually got to pressing the pieces for me, her handling was remarkably light and efficient.

I mouthed, *Thank you.*

She held a palm out for payment, then giggled at the

look on my face. "Just teasing. I'm Rosalind. Rose," she whispered.

Hearing a name instead of a number was like pulling on a ribbon bow to unwrap a precious gift.

"Ella."

"I'm not really a princess."

"Me neither."

"Just a countess." Rose grinned.

Marta coughed. Back to work.

Every few minutes I sneaked a peek at Rabbit. She was sewing with her whole body bent over in focus. She'd let the blouse seams out fine but she'd tacked the sleeves back in *the wrong way around*. They were bent as if the arms were broken.

"Hey!" I didn't know her name (and she probably wouldn't answer to Rabbit). "Hey, you?" She looked up.

Then it hit me. Marta's warning: *There's only room for one of you.*

It had to be me. I was *not* going to swill around in the mud outside like the others, just a nameless one of many. I had skills. Talent. Ambition. Didn't I *deserve* to have a decent job and a chance to rise? Grandma wouldn't want me to go under. She'd be waiting for me back home. Rabbit would have to fend for herself. So I looked away from the botched blouse and shook my head—*It's nothing.*

Rabbit carried on wrecking her work. I got pleats pressed on my dress, put in a side zip, and started hand-sewing the neatest neckline ever. My head drooped lower and lower. It would be so easy just to close my eyes and snooze for a while. When was the last time I'd slept properly? More than three weeks ago. Maybe a little doze wouldn't hurt . . .

Someone jostled me awake. How long had I slept? I glanced around. Rose the squirrel was just going past me. She mouthed, *Nearly four.*

Nearly four! I hustled back into action. I was still picking off tacking threads as Marta approached.

"Well, ladies, how was your first — and probably your last — day at work here? Show me the dress, schoolgirl."

I shook it out and handed it over. It was a mess. A rag. A dishcloth of a gown. The *worst* thing ever sewn in the history of dressmaking. I was aware that the other workers were watching. I couldn't breathe.

In silence Marta scrutinized every inch of the emerald silk. In silence she held it up and shook and shimmered it.

"How about that?" she said eventually. "You *can* sew. Quite well too. I should know. I trained in all the very best places."

She snapped her fingers for the blouse next. Rabbit-woman was so stiff with fear her hands could barely uncurl from the cloth. She noticed her terrible mistake with the sleeves at exactly the same moment as Marta did.

"I'm sorry, I'm sorry." Rabbit panicked. "I know . . . the sleeves . . . the wrong way round . . . I can put them right. I won't do it again, I swear. Please let me stay."

21

Marta's voice was low and dangerous. "I told you how it was—only room for one of you. Isn't that right, schoolgirl?"

My heart was thudding. I wanted to explain it had just been an accident—the woman was tired, nervous, not at her best. The words stuck in my throat, like they do in a dream when you need to call for help. I unraveled with shame inside, but said nothing.

"It was an accident," came a timid voice. "She says she won't do it again."

Squirrel was hovering just behind Marta, small, watchful, ready to dart away.

Marta ignored Rose, as if she truly had been a rodent squeaking. "Get out, you idiot!" she shouted at Rabbit. "Or do I need to throw you out?" She raised her hand and took a step forward. The dark figure at the end of the room shifted and stretched.

Bleached white from fear, Rabbit scurried to the door and disappeared. We all just watched, semisafe in our sanctuary.

When the door to outside had closed again, Marta blew out a breath that said, *Don't you all realize how hard my life is?*

Next she took my green dress and headed for another door at the far end of the sewing room. That had to be the fitting room. My client, Carla, would try the dress and then I'd know if I had a job or not.

I whispered to Frog, "What . . . what will happen to her? That woman who just left?"

Frog never looked up from her apple-green wool. "Who knows? Maybe the same as Rhoda, the woman whose place you're hoping to take."

I waited. Frog said nothing else. She continued sewing, stitch after stitch. Marta came out of the fitting room. My eyes followed her as she slowly wove her way, sharklike, through the tables toward me. I stood up so quickly my stool fell over.

"*Pins!*" she commanded.

I scrabbled on the table. Marta opened her pin box and I counted twenty pins back in. Next she collected every remnant of fabric and paper. Frog scowled — no chance of getting my paper scraps now. I wondered what she wanted them for.

Marta looked me up and down. Coming under her scrutiny was like having your soul scrubbed with one of those wiry green pan scourers. Finally, reluctantly, she put me out of my misery.

"The client says the dress is enchanting."

I sagged with relief.

"As a reward, she gave me this. One of the perks of the job — extra food." Marta unfolded a packet of paper. It contained a slice of hard brown bread spread with a measly layer of margarine. Twice the size of my usual supper ration.

Unbelievably, I was too twisted up inside to eat. "Er, thank you, I'm not hungry."

"Liar! You've had — what? A mug of brown coffee-water

23

for breakfast, and you'll get a mug of brown soup-water for supper. You're hungry enough to overcome stupid fits of conscience about that dopey bungler I booted out. Hungry enough to do whatever it takes to survive here."

She knew I'd noticed Rabbit's mistake. She knew why I'd said nothing. She approved.

Right there in front of me, Marta ate the entire piece of bread and licked her fingers. She said, "Watch and learn, *Ella*, watch and learn."

If I slept at all that night, it was to dream of green dresses, wafting past in a parade of loveliness.

People laugh at fashion. *It's just clothes*, they say.

Just clothes. Except, not one of the people I've heard mock fashion was naked at the time. They all got dressed in the morning, picking clothes that said, *Hey, I'm a successful banker*. Or, *I'm a busy mother*. Or, *I'm a tired teacher . . . a decorated soldier . . . a pompous judge . . . a cheeky barmaid . . . a truck driver, a nurse . . .* Clothes show who you are, or who you want to be.

People might say, *Why do you take clothes so seriously, when there are more important things to worry about, like the War?*

I was worried about the War all right. The War got in the way of everything. Out in the real world, outside of here, I'd wasted hours lining up at shops with empty shelves. More hours hiding in the cellar when bombers flew over. I'd put up with endless news updates, and Grandad plotting battle lines on a map pinned to the kitchen wall. I'd known War would come—it was all people talked about for months.

It was War that brought me to Birchwood—known, in a harsher language, as Auschwitz-Birkenau. The place where everyone arrives, and nobody leaves.

Here people find out that clothes aren't so trivial after all. The first thing They did when we arrived was make us strip. Minutes off the train and we were sorted into male and female. They shoved us into a room and told us to undress. Right there. With everyone watching. Not even underwear allowed.

Our clothes were folded into piles. Without them we weren't bankers, teachers, nurses, barmaids, or truck drivers anymore. We were scared and humiliated.

Just clothes.

I'd stared at my pile of folded clothes. I memorized the soft wool of my sweater. It was my favorite green sweater, embroidered with cherries, a birthday present from Grandma. I memorized the neat folds of my trousers and my socks, rolled into a pair. My bra, too—my first-ever bra!—that I'd hidden from view along with my knickers.

Next They took our hair. All our hair. Shaved it off with blunt razors. Gave us limp triangles of cloth as headscarves. Made us pick out shoes from a pile about as high as a house. I'd found a pair. Rose obviously hadn't been so lucky, with her one silk shoe and her one leather brogue.

They said we'd get our clothes back after a shower. They

lied. We got sack dresses with stripes. As Stripeys we ran around like herds of panicked zebras. We weren't people anymore. They could do what they liked to us.

So don't tell me clothes don't matter.

I turned up at the workshop the next day, bleary-eyed from a predawn start. I was oh so ready to get dressmaking . . . only to find I was ordered to polish the fitting-room floor.

"I thought I was here to sew, not scrub," I complained to Marta.

The slap came too fast to avoid. One hard palm, on the side of my face that wasn't yet bruised. I was so surprised I almost lifted a hand to hit back.

Marta's eyes glinted as if she knew what I was thinking. This was about showing who was boss. Fine. She was.

I washed, put on a brown coverall, and collected polishing gear. Rose wasn't anywhere to be seen. Too soft to stick it out in the sewing room, obviously. Her sort were all very nice, but they had no backbone. Not that it mattered to me, of course. I wasn't here to make friends.

When I opened the door to the fitting room, I stood there openmouthed. Birchwood was so bare, so stark, I'd almost forgotten there could be *nice* things in a room.

For starters, there was a lovely bobble-trim on the lampshades . . . and real lamps, not just bare light bulbs protected by wire cages. There was an armchair in one corner. An *actual* armchair, with braiding and a grass-green cushion. Such a fat cushion! If I were a cat I'd curl up on it and only wake up when someone set out a saucer of cream.

Pretty cotton curtains hid the view from the windows. Peony-patterned paper covered concrete walls. Around the fitting stage in the center of the room, there were real woven rugs and a parade of dressmaker mannequins.

Most decadent of all, there was a mirror.

It was a fantastic, full-length tilted mirror, the frame painted white with gold scrolling. The sort of mirror that would stand in the fitting room of the finest city fashion house. I could imagine myself in such a place, padding across soft carpets to see how good my gowns looked on ridiculously rich clients. There'd be a waiting list for my creations, of course. Minions scurrying to do my bidding. And silver trays with pots of tea and plates of pink cakes — those tiny cakes made of fluff and icing sugar . . .

"Hello, Ella."

A voice broke my daydream. Turning, I caught a view of myself in the mirror. What a scarecrow! Ugly clothes, stupid shoes, bruised face. No glamorous accessories, only flannel cleaning mitts, a yellow duster, and a tin of polish. Standing next to me in the reflection was Squirrel-girl, Rosalind, holding a bucket of steamy hot water. Her sleeves were rolled up, and her dainty hands were raw red.

"I'm on window-cleaning duty!" she said brightly, as if it was a treat. "Except I can't get to the top panes."

She was a bit of a shorty. I was tall for my age, which was

how I could pass for sixteen. Tall but not at all curvy. Even before the mouse-sized rations here, I'd struggled to fill a bra. School skirts always threatened to slip off my straight hips even though I ate and ate and ate.

Grandma reassured me I'd fill out. "Wait till you hit forty," she said. "That's when I got big."

There weren't many women aged forty or older in Birchwood. Those who were looked eighty. Youth was stronger—lasted longer. As long as you weren't too young: sixteen minimum, just as Rose had prompted me the day before. Otherwise . . .

Then I forgot all about Rose and Unthinkable Things. I'd spotted a pile of fashion magazines. *World of Fashion* and *Fashion Forecast Monthly*. They were exactly the same ones sold at my newsstand back home. The shopkeeper—a twitchy little hamster of a woman with jangly gold earrings—always kept back a copy of each title for me and Grandma.

Back home, Grandma and I used to spend hours reading these magazines, forgetting all about War as we turned the pages together.

"Seams too close together on the back of that," Grandma would say, stabbing a picture, or, "put *those* pockets on *that* dress and you've got a stunner." Or both at the same time we'd chorus, "What a disgusting color!" or "What a gorgeous outfit!" Then she would make coffee in little china cups—not quite as strong as the way Grandad liked it—and she'd pour something into hers from a smoky green bottle on the top shelf of the pantry, "to add a little zing," she'd confess.

Water droplets splashed on the magazine covers. Rose was wobbling with her bucket, up on the edge of the armchair.

"Sorry!" she sang out.

Sorry doesn't butter any bread, my grandma says.

"I could . . ."

"Would you? Thank you!" Rose jumped down and passed me the bucket.

I had been going to say, *I could hold the chair*, but Rose assumed I was offering to clean the window glass for her. As if! The last thing I wanted to do was see outside this safe haven. The only view from the windows would be of watchtowers poised like storks along wire fences. And chimneys. Smoking chimneys.

When I was done Rose smiled and said thank you. I shrugged and went to pull the rugs up, still thinking of the wonderful pictures in *Fashion Forecast*. They gave me so many ideas for new frocks. If I cleaned well, would Marta let me sew again? Sewing was my love in life. Also, if I sewed there might be more rewards. I'd been so *stupid* not taking that bread the day before. Cleaning could mean sewing *plus* food. Perfect.

I knelt to start polishing. I quickly got a nice technique going — hands in mitts, circle with the right hand, circle with the left.

"You don't do it like that," said Rose, putting her bucket down.

Her cultured voice cut my confidence. She had to be faking the posh accent to make the rest of us feel like yokels.

I scowled at her. "I thought you were a *countess*. If you were, you'd have an army of servants to do it for you."

"Not an army — but quite a few."

"So you're rich?"

"I was."

"Lucky you."

She spread her hands as if to say, *See how lucky I am.* "I still know how to polish a floor better than you. Watch this . . ."

Off came her stupid mismatched shoes. On went a spare pair of mitts. On her *feet*.

Right there in the middle of the fitting-room floor, Rose started doing a soft-shoe shuffle. Shimmy to the right, shimmy to the left. Hip wiggle here, bottom wiggle there. She snapped her fingers and began to hum oh so very quietly. I knew the tune! Grandma used to sing it in the sewing room, tapping her slippers to the beat.

"*Rose!*" I warned. "What if someone hears you?"

She giggled. Unbelievably, I giggled too. Suddenly she shot off like an ice skater, right around the fitting stage in the center of the room, past the mirror, and up to where I was kneeling.

"May I have this dance?" she asked, with a princely bow.

"Are you crazy?" I hissed.

She shrugged her little squirrel shoulders. "Probably the sanest person in this place, m'dear. Care to waltz?"

Waltz? Here?

The way Rose looked, so bold and playful, I actually couldn't resist. I pretended to simper at the invitation, then rose up gracefully to join her. Well, maybe not *gracefully*. I still had polish mitts on my hands. Copying Rose, I put them on my feet. Forgetting everything else, we danced around the fitting-room floor, humming and giggling at the same time. We were princesses in a fairy tale! We were glamour goddesses in a glitzy ritzy nightclub! We were beauty queens in a pageant!

We were caught.

Footsteps crunched the gravel path to the outer door. There was someone in the doorway with a face so flat it could have been painted on. Rose and I froze, as if caught in a spell. There was no time to grovel. No time to erase our existence from the room. A client had arrived.

She was tall, with solid yellow hair and lips like sulky cushions. She had a heavy tread. Her boots left prints on the newly polished floor. The bobbles on the lampshade trembled. So did I.

She fixed us with a gaze that had us pinned to the wall like butterflies in a collection case, then she strode into the room. She set her gloves on the magazines and her hat on the armchair. Her whip went in the corner near the door.

Here we were, in a prison camp for innocents, run by criminals.

And here was one of the guards.

31

* * *

All my life I'd dreamed of owning a dress shop. When I should've been out playing with other kids or at the very least doing schoolwork, I was sitting cross-legged on the floor of Grandma's workroom, making miniatures of the gowns going under her machine needle. My dolls even discussed the décor of fantasy fitting rooms (I did all the voices) then posed in their precocious fashions.

Now I was in an actual fitting room, with an *actual client*, and I turned into a rabbit, just like the woman yesterday. But rabbits are easy prey for dogs, foxes, and wolves, especially when they're wearing polishing mitts on their feet. Quickly I whipped the mitts off and put on my stupid wooden shoes.

"Hello, I'm Carla!" breezed the client. Her accent was stodgy, how a potato would sound if it could talk. She was nothing like the bored block of a guard in the sewing room — that dark figure watching over us. Carla was young and bursting with energy, like the boisterous girls I used to see in gangs on the streets back home, who've just left school to start their first job.

"Yes, I'm early!" she exclaimed. "I just *had* to try on my new dress again. Have you seen it? The green silk. I *love* it. So stylish. So chic." She pronounced it *chick*. "Just *enchanting*. Won't everyone be jealous when they see what I'm wearing?"

She unbuttoned her jacket and held it out to me. Wordlessly, I took it. Where was I supposed to put it?

The door to the workshop burst open and in came Marta, as if pulled on wheels. She braked and blustered, "Excuse me, ma'am. I'm so sorry — we didn't expect you so soon." She snapped her fingers at Rose. "You! Get the dress."

To me she hissed, "Straighten the rugs!"

Carla carried on talking as she undressed. "Such a lovely spring day again. The mornings are lighter, aren't they? I do hate getting up in the dark, don't you? Here . . ."

I was given her skirt to hold too.

In slip and stockings Carla stepped up onto the fitting stage in the center of the room. She admired herself in that amazing mirror. There was plenty of her to admire. She was rounded in all the right places, unlike me. My hips were so narrow they'd just about fit in a toaster like a slice of bread.

Rose came back in with the dress. *My dress.* I almost sighed as it slipped over Carla's up-reached arms and ran like water over her tummy and rump. It touched exactly where it should and swished beautifully as she turned this way and that in front of the mirror. Grandma would be proud of my creation.

Carla beamed at her reflection and clapped her hands like a kid in a cake shop. "Oh, you are so clever. Such neat stitching. Such a flattering design — how did you do it?"

"I —"

I got no further. Marta glared at me — *silence.*

"Years of practice," Marta murmured. "It helps to have a client with such a good figure. I knew this style would suit you, and I picked this shade especially for spring. Silk *is* difficult to work with, but the effect is worth it, I'm sure you'll agree. I did train in all the very best places."

Marta went around the hem of the skirt, checking it was level, front and back. Something fell. She snapped her fingers at me: *pin!* I crouched down and swept the floor — with the back of my hand, like Grandma had taught me to do — until I felt the pin. Grandma had a saying: *See a pin, pick it up, all that day have good luck.* Hearing Marta take credit for *my* work, I could happily have jabbed that pin into her arm. Instead I handed it back.

"The dress will be *wonderful* for the concert at the end of the week," said Carla. "All those violins — it's not my thing, but I want to look pretty, of course. And thanks to you, I will."

"I'll have the hem done in an hour," Marta said, straightening up and admiring "her" work.

"Ye-es . . ." Carla stopped posturing and glared into the mirror.

Marta frowned. "Is something wrong?"

I had an urge to step forward and say, *Yes, there's something wrong! That's my dress you're taking credit for!* Plus, if I'd had the nerve, I'd've added that there was absolutely nothing wrong with the dress.

Carla clapped her hands once more. "I've got it! Bigger pads in the shoulders — that'll really add some oomph. And a belt. A nice polka-dot belt. I saw a picture you could copy in one of those magazines there. And a pussycat bow at the neckline perhaps? Or would that be too much?"

Grandma often came home from a fitting with one of her ladies complaining they had less sense of style than a loo brush, but what could you do? As long as they paid up on time, you did what they asked, she'd say. Then she'd give a little shiver and add, *But you don't have to like it.*

Birchwood, it seemed, wasn't much different. Marta nodded at every single one of these gruesome suggestions.

Carla maybe caught my expression. Her eyes narrowed as she looked from me to Marta. There was a kind of cunning in her look, even if she did act like a dimwit farm girl who's found fame and fortune. I could see that Carla had realized Marta was lying about who had made the dress.

"Wait!" she cried. "Forget all that. Make . . . a matching jacket . . ." She squinted at me, searching for approval. Whatever she saw gave her the confidence to go on. "Yes, a jacket. Three-quarter sleeves, bolero style, lined, and maybe embroidered. With your talent, it'll be a breeze. Good, that's settled then. Quick, take this off. I have to be back at work now. Duty calls!"

She put on the uniform once more, then off she went, slapping her whip handle against her booted leg and humming a dance tune.

"Don't say a word!" Marta jabbed a bony finger into my chest the second the door shut and we were alone.

"But—"

"Not a word!"

"You—"

"Oh, *fine*. You're cross because that big pig thinks *I* made her dress, not you?"

"Well, yes . . ."

"Tough. You do what you have to do to survive, understand?"

I nodded slowly. I was learning fast.

I blurted out, "When can I send a message to let my grandma know I'm OK? She's been ill this spring, and Grandad's not much use looking after her. I was on my way back from school when I got rounded up and brought here. She will be worried sick about me."

Marta sighed. "You really are green, aren't you? How long have you been here?"

"Three weeks."

"No wonder you're so clueless. It is a bit of a shock, I'll give you that." She reached into her overall pocket and retrieved a cardboard box. When she shook it, out came two skinny cigarettes.

"Here. Take them. And make me a bolero jacket for Carla."

"Thanks, but I don't smoke."

"Like I said—*clueless*! You don't *smoke* cigarettes at Birchwood, they're *money*. Buy some food or friends; it's all the same to me."

"And getting a message out . . . ?"

36

"Not a hope. Not for a factory full of smokes. You think They want the rest of the world knowing this place exists? Take my advice, schoolgirl—forget your family. Forget everything out there. Here, there's only one person in the world to worry about: the big *me, myself, I.* Any time you're stuck wondering how to act, ask yourself, *What would Marta do?* and it'll see you right."

I stared at the pinched-up rolls of paper with shreds of brown tobacco hanging out of the ends. Grandad used to roll his own cigarettes. He had nimble fingers like mine, but his were stained from the tobacco. When he coughed at night, which he did a lot, I used to creep to his cigarette pouch and flush the contents down the toilet. In the morning he'd laugh at me, ruffle up my hair, then send me out to buy more. I hated cigarettes. Their smoke makes fabric stink.

"Well?" Marta looked straight at me, sizing me up.

I took the cigarettes.

It wasn't all I took from the fitting room that morning.

"Ella. Hey, Ella!"

I was miles away, figuring out how to notch the lapels of Carla's bolero jacket so they'd fit nicely. Grandma could've shown me easy as pie. Easy as steak pie, cherry pie, peach pie, apple pie . . . My mouth started watering.

Grandma wasn't here. Thankfully.

It was Rose.

"What's the matter?" I whispered back.

"You have to stop now. It's nearly time for supper."

She said it like there was a big table with a starched white linen cloth and candlesticks and napkins in silver rings, and massive plates piled high with steaming food, just waiting for us to gorge on. Maybe it had been like that in her posh princess palace.

"Just a minute," I grouched. "I need to figure this out."

Annoyingly, Rose didn't move. She reached for the jacket and turned the collar one way then another. "You could just make small snips *here* to release the tension; then the lapels will sit better."

I blinked. *Of course.* I was an idiot not to have thought of that. I called, "Scissors!"

I made the snips. The lapels finally stopped fighting me.

At the tables all around, girls and women were folding away work and returning their allocation of pins. They moved slowly, rubbing sore shoulder and neck muscles, stretching out with their hands in the small of their backs. It had been a long day. Exhausting. Even so, nobody wanted to break the spell of safety by leaving. Outside, dogs were barking.

"Shove off, *Princess*," said Marta, appearing suddenly. Rose curtsied and did just that.

Marta poked my work with her long fingers. "Not bad. The client asked for embellishment. Can you embroider?"

Could I embroider? Good question. Marta tapped her foot, waiting for the answer.

What would Marta do?

Lie.

"I'm really good at embroidery," I said.

"Marvelous. Do a butterfly or flowers — something nice and easy."

Off she went. I sighed. I hated embroidery. Stupid satin stitch and fiddly knots.

I kept a lookout for Rose over supper, but she was lost among the thousands and thousands of women in striped clothing slurping soup-water from tin bowls. It was sheer chance that I found her, not long before lights-out at nine p.m. I was in my block, up on my bunk. The barrack blocks were long, low, miserable buildings. About five hundred of us were squashed inside each block. We were wedged into damp wooden shelves, three tiers of them, reaching floor to ceiling. Each shelf was divided into bunks with rows of dirty straw mattresses. At least six to a bunk, at least two to a mattress. There was no other furniture, unless you counted the toilet buckets. That night my usual bunkmate hadn't turned up. I didn't ask why not. Some questions you don't want answers to.

I heard a kerfuffle down at floor level and peered over the edge of the bunk. The barrack boss and her cronies had Rose cornered. I hadn't even realized she was in my block. Too bad she'd caught the attention of the boss. Barrack bosses were prominents, like Marta at the workshop. They were prisoners, but they acted like guards. They got the best food, best bunks, and best jobs. Our barrack boss was a woman named Gerda. She was so sturdy her nickname quickly became *Girder*. Her muscly arms could well have been made of welded metal. She slung these big arms around a different girlfriend every day of the week. She boasted a really low number, which meant she must've been in Birchwood for several years, not weeks. Nobody soft could survive that long.

Rose was soft. Girder & Co. had her cornered near the stove in the middle of the hut. They weren't being rough — yet. They were just teasing. Testing how far they could go.

"Got nowhere to sleep, little one?" Girder mocked. "Aw, don't cry. You don't want to spoil that pretty face . . ."

Rose wasn't crying. She was just standing there looking helpless, letting them jostle her. Hadn't she learned *anything* since coming to Birchwood? You couldn't let people push you around. I bet Marta never got bullied in *her* barrack. She was probably boss there too.

What would Marta do?

Ignore Rose. Join in with the bullying. Side with Girder.

I didn't want to get in Girder's bad books. As boss, she supervised the slicing and sharing of the daily bread ration. She also doled out duties, such as lugging the soup cauldron . . . or the toilet bucket. Girder blew a cloud of cigarette smoke in Rose's face. I could guess what would come next — a cigarette burn somewhere tender. Best not to interfere.

On the other hand, wouldn't it be better to have Rose as bunkmate, rather than sleeping next to another complete stranger?

"Hey. Rose! Rosalind! Up here!" I patted the thin straw mattress of my bunk.

Rose broke into a smile brighter than the single bulb dangling between the beds. She waved and made a little gesture for Girder & Co. to step aside. They were so surprised that they actually let her through.

"Thank you," she said, as if they were all guests mingling at some tea party. Despite having arms as thin as noodles, she managed to haul herself up to the third tier of the bunks. Girder flicked her skirt up a few times as she was climbing, just to save face. I got lost in a quick reverie about noodles with fresh basil leaves and a rich tomato sauce . . . the sort of meal you just had to slurp, then you'd get saucy flecks all around your mouth . . .

"Phew! Don't you get altitude sickness?" Rose said, heaving herself onto the mattress.

"Watch your head—"

Too late. Rose knocked her skull. The ceiling was very low, too low even to sit with a straight spine.

I shifted to make room for her. "The air's fresher up here." *Fresh* meant freezing when the wind blew through all the cracks and gaps. "And people don't climb over you all night to go to the toilet bucket. On the flip side, if you need to pee, it's a long way down in the dark."

41

"Thanks for letting me share," Rose said, rubbing her head. "Some other women took my bunk space. It wasn't as classy as this."

"*Classy?*"

She grinned. "Well, *we're* here, aren't we?"

Now that I had company, I was in a bit of a dilemma. I'd swapped one of the cigarettes from Marta for an extra slice of bread and marg. How was I supposed to eat it with Rose watching? I supposed I could hide it till breakfast, assuming nobody stole it while I was asleep, or rats didn't get at it. The rats that ran across the roof beams were fatter than any of the humans in the beds below.

Hunger got the better of me. I pulled the bread out from inside my dress and started nibbling the crust. Rose swallowed . . . then politely turned away. I chewed as quietly as I could. It was no use.

"Here. Have some," I said.

"Me? Oh, I'm full," she lied. "Couldn't manage another mouthful."

"Don't be stupid . . ."

"Well, if you insist."

We munched together. The difference was, I picked and ate crumbs from the front of my dress. Rose acted all polite and swept them away.

Next I contorted myself to take my stupid shoes off. Apart from the fact they gave me horrible bloated blisters, they were the closest thing I had to a pillow.

Rose tilted her head, just like a squirrel testing a nut to see if it was sound or bad. "Can you hear rustling?"

"It's rats."

She shook her head. "Not rats, or bedbugs."

When I moved to get less uncomfortable she said, "It's you! *You're* rustling."

"I'm not!"

"You are—you're positively crackling."

"It's your imagination."

"If you say so."

I scowled. "Who says rustling's a crime? I can rustle as much as I like."

"Absolutely. But if *I* found out you'd taken one of the fashion magazines from the fitting room, someone else might too."

Red with embarrassment, I pulled the copy of *Fashion Forecast Monthly* out of my sleeve, where it had been rolled all day.

Rose raised an eyebrow. "You know what They'll do if They catch you with it?"

I didn't know *precisely* what the punishment would be; just that it would be bad.

"Oh, come on—it's just one magazine," I blustered.

"It's still stealing."

"It's called *organizing* here."

"It's still stealing."

"So?"

"Weren't you taught that stealing's *wrong*?"

I almost laughed out loud at that. *Of course* I knew stealing was wrong. I never took a single penny of Grandad's tobacco money on my way to the shop. I never pilfered so much as a spool of thread from Grandma's sewing box. There was one time she caught me with her purse and she gave me a monster lecture on respecting people's property, even though I tried to tell her I just wanted to play with it. That was true. It was a big leather crocodile of a purse with snap fasteners on the outside, gut-red lining, and a rusty zip on the change pocket. Crocodiles were fast, tough, and capable of eating anything.

I said, "They stole everything off me when I got here. That was wrong too. Anyway, are you going to tell on me?"

"Of course not!" Rose said scornfully. There was a pause, before she asked in her oh-so-upper-class accent, "Aren't you going to look at it before you give it back?"

"*If* I give it back."

I passed Rose the magazine. She stroked the front cover. "My mama used to despair at my reading this *rag*, as she called it. Said I'd be better off reading good books, or writing my own."

"Your mother called *Fashion Forecast Monthly* a *rag*? It's got design reviews, editorials, the letters page, and sketches and photos . . ."

"I know!" laughed Rose. "In full, glorious color! Isn't it all so *brown* here?"

"Lights-out!" yelled Girder.

From brown to black: darkness. So much for a fashion

fix. I was now terrified I'd be found out as a thief, hauled from my bunk and . . . and what the guards did next wouldn't be good. So far Carla was the only Birchwood guard who seemed halfway human.

Quietly: "Hey, Rose . . . thanks for the tip about the jacket lapels today."

"You're welcome."

"Where'd you learn to sew?"

"Me? Oh, a lady came to the palace and I had lessons with her. When I was little I dreamed of having a dress shop. Or a bookshop. Or a zoo—I was quite fickle."

I shifted in the straw. Rose couldn't have a dress shop! That was *my* plan! And how silly she was, pretending she'd lived in a palace.

"Ella?" Rose whispered a few minutes later.

"What?"

"Good night."

"You too."

"Sleep well."

Fat chance.

A pause.

"Ella, shall I tell you a bedtime story?"

"No."

Another pause.

"Ella?"

I turned over on the lumpy straw. "What now?"

"I'm glad you're here," came Rose's voice in the darkness. "Bread's good, but friends are better."

45

* * *

I couldn't sleep. It wasn't just the ghost of a guilty conscience about stealing—I mean *organizing*—the magazine. It wasn't just hunger either. No, I couldn't sleep because Rose snored. Not great gasping, snorting snores like my grandad, in the next bedroom back home. Rose did little snuffly snores that would be cute if she weren't lying right next to me.

What would Marta do?

Poke her in the ribs.

"Mm, tickles," Rose murmured, without waking up.

I lay awake, refusing to think about anything except what I'd sew in the morning.

The whistle blew at four thirty a.m., same as every day. We all scrambled down from our bunks to run for roll call. There was a roll call morning and evening. All Stripeys had to be counted to make sure we hadn't vanished into thin air, or something equally improbable, such as escaping. The guards had Lists. There were no names on the Lists. Names would have meant we were human. Stripeys had numbers.

Stripeys had badges, too, made of colored cloth sewn onto our dresses. The badge you had showed exactly why They had decided you weren't fit to live in the real world anymore.

Most bosses had green triangles. That meant they'd been criminals even before they came to Birchwood. Rose's badge was a red triangle, which told everyone she was a political enemy. How could such a dreamy dipstick be considered a political threat? Obviously They didn't like book readers. They didn't like people of my religion either. Worshipping the wrong god meant you got a star. It was like the gold stars we used to get at school for good work, only this star meant you were the absolute lowest of the low. Most Stripeys had the star. Starred prisoners were treated worst of all.

I hated the star. I hated the badges, and the Lists too.

It wasn't dramatic at first, out in the real world. It began with little things. Last to be picked for sports at school (because *Your Sort aren't good in teams*). Graded worse on exams (*You and Your Sort must've copied from each other to get so many answers right*). Ignored at the back of the class, when my hand was up (*Does anyone know the answer? Anyone? Anyone? Anyone?*).

Little things became big things. In science class the teacher made a boy stand at the front while his head was measured. "Look at his color!" the teacher mocked. "And the skull measurements are clear—he's from the *wrong* race. Utterly inferior."

I squirmed at my desk but didn't dare say anything in case *I* got called up.

At school assembly one morning the head teacher announced, *The following pupils must now stand and leave the premises* . . . He had a List. My name was on it. I have never, ever felt so embarrassed as when walking out of the auditorium with hundreds of eyes watching. When I got home, Grandad threatened to go flush the head's head down a toilet. I went to a new school instead. One only for people on Lists.

It got worse. Houses and shops and synagogues vandalized. Books burned. Neighbors taken away at night in trucks with bars instead of windows.

Ignore all that nonsense, Grandma used to tell me. *It's just bullying, and you can't give in to bullies. There's nothing wrong with who we are.*

If there was nothing wrong with us, how come we'd ended up in a prison like this?

Here in Birchwood, the main thing was to be on a List for *work*. If you didn't work, you didn't live. Simple as that.

Roll call was the worst thing ever, especially in predawn darkness. Stripeys lined up in rows of five to be counted by the bosses. If anyone was late, the count began again. If anyone was missing—again. If anyone collapsed from hunger or tiredness or the cold (or all three)—again began the count. Yawning guards clustered together, wrapped in black cloaks. That morning, I thought I saw Carla, off in the distance, smoking, with a great black dog panting at her side.

Rose was at my side. When no Bosses were near she suddenly whispered, "I can embroider. If you like, I'll sew ivy sprays on the lapels of the green jacket you're making."

I glanced over. "Really? Are you any good?"

Rose stuck her tongue out at me. It was so unexpected

I almost laughed out loud, and *that* would have been lethal. Laughing wasn't allowed at roll call. (Technically talking wasn't either, but this was frock-talk, and therefore irresistible.)

"Sorry, I mean, *thank you*," I whispered. "Ivy's nice. My grandma once had to embroider white satin ivy leaves on a wedding dress. It's supposed to symbolize marriage, because it twines and clings."

"And it's poisonous," Rose said, with a glint in her eyes.

I meant to put the pilfered copy of *Fashion Forecast Monthly* back, truly I did. The trouble was, the fitting room was endlessly busy that day, with clients having final tweaks to their concert frocks. At one point the door to the fitting room opened, and I could see right through. A short, mature woman was being shown clothes modeled by the giraffe I'd met on my first day. Her real name was Shona. The older woman was wearing a grass-green wool crêpe dress, so she definitely wasn't a guard. Marta seemed to be treating her like some kind of goddess.

"Who's that?" I asked Frog, whose real name was Francine. Froggy Francine was good at sewing bulky fabrics and plain stitching.

"You don't know who *that* is?" Francine whistled under her breath. "Sweetheart, she's the reason we're all here. She's Madam H."

"Who?"

"Only the commandant's *wife*! A real fashion lover!

49

Started out with a couple of seamstresses working in her attic — her home's just on the edge of Birchwood — then she set up this workshop so all the officers' wives and the guards could have fancy clothes. They got jealous, see, with her always looking so smart. That lad's one of her kiddies."

I looked again and saw a little boy. That was enough to make me gawk. You never saw children here. *Never.* He was dressed in neatly pressed shorts and shirt. His hair was combed and parted. His shoes were gleaming.

The boy squinted through the open door at us. Francine mimed pulling a throttling rope around her neck. The boy backed away and hid in his mother's skirts.

"One day they'll all hang for what they've done to us," Francine muttered. "Father, mother, the whole rotten family."

She must've seen the look on my face. "He's just a kid!" I said.

"So are you, sweetheart. So are all the kiddies that go up the chimneys — *pouf!*"

At first when I heard about people going up the chimneys, I thought they were being made to clean them. Much as I wanted to carry on believing that, there was too much smoke, too much ash. Too many people who arrived and vanished.

Don't think about it. Think dresses.

I held fast to the image of smart Madam H., the most important client in this universe. I memorized her face, her coloring, and her figure. Right there and then I decided I'd make clothes for her one day. Dressmakers need a prestigious client list. Otherwise you ended up dressing whoever comes through the door.

The door to the fitting room closed completely. Too risky to try and put the magazine back now. I figured if no one had missed it, I might as well keep it. Why shouldn't I? It was none of Rose's business what I did. None at all. I didn't care what she thought, either.

I did remember that Francine had asked for scraps of pattern-cutting paper, back on my first day. When the guard at the end of the room wasn't looking, I carefully tore a page of ads from the magazine. They were for things I'd almost forgotten existed. Perfume. Soap. High-heeled shoes. That made me think of Grandma taking me shopping just before the new school term. She'd been wearing sensible block heels, a little worn down at the sides. I was in my boring school shoes. That didn't stop me from ogling the sparkle of evening shoes covered in sequins and diamanté.

"Fine feathers butter no parsnips," she'd muttered. Whatever that meant.

I'd heard tantalizing rumors of some sort of shop in Birchwood. They called it the Department Store. They said it was a *land of plenty*.

Anyway, while Marta was busy bullying some other seam-stress, I poked Francine under the table.

Did you still want paper? I mouthed.

Francine raised her eyes to the ceiling and mouthed a very big *thank you!* I passed her the page, hoping she wouldn't mind it was only the ads.

The ungrateful lump never even looked at what was printed on the sheet. She tore it into four, heaved herself off her stool, and headed for the toilet, waving the paper as if it was some kind of award she'd won. When she came back from the lavatory, the paper was nowhere to be seen.

So much for generosity.

Yellow

One memory: Rose jumping down off our bunk, crying, "Life, life, life!" She put her arms in the air and whirled around and around till we were all dizzy watching. "I love being able to move! I love breathing! I love bread! I could just kiss everything and marry everyone!"

Girder chewed her evening ration thoughtfully. "Well, she's cracked, that's for sure."

Spring mud turned into summer dust.

We baked.

I'd always hated the last few days of the summer term at school. We'd be bent over our desks, sleeves rolled up, clothes stuck to our backs with sweat as sunshine taunted us outside. Then came liberation—the last school bell! Tumbling into the street in a jumble of books, bikes, and happiness . . . weeks and weeks of freedom ahead!

There was no liberation in Birchwood. Every morning, whistle-woken, we lined up in fives for roll call. By summer it was hot even at dawn. We burned in our thin dresses, with nothing but a triangle of cotton on our cropped heads. Guards moved slowly among us. They were like crows settling on a field of stubble to glean insects. They checked that our numbers tallied, that our badges were sewn on right, and that we all looked fit for work. Just like crows, they kept their eye out for treats: Stripeys who needed punishing. The guards pounced on anyone who stood out from the crowd. I saw a woman beaten unconscious because she'd dared to slick her tufty hair with spit so it looked a tiny bit more stylish.

Sometimes Carla came by with her dog, Pippa. It panted and choked to get ahead. A yank from the leash and Pippa came to heel.

At roll call, Carla ignored me. In the fitting room, she boasted to me about her suntan. I made her a lemon-yellow sundress—which Marta once again took credit for. Carla knew Marta was lying, I was sure of it. She said, "Do you reckon *Marta* could make me a swimsuit?"

"I'm sure *Marta* could," I answered demurely.

By then I was trusted to be alone with clients in the fitting room—no more floor washing and grunt work for me! I sewed until my hands cramped and my eyes blurred. It was harder than anything I'd ever done before. My original career plan had been to learn skills with Grandma at home, then somehow save up to go to a trade college for extra finesse. After that I'd start at the bottom, in a dress business, and work my way up to owning my own shop.

I wasn't at home with Grandma, but I was still learning skills. Marta was surprisingly helpful when it came to teaching tailoring tricks.

"I did train in all the very best places," she said over and over.

Yet Carla wanted *me* to make her new clothes, not Marta.

In the fitting room one day, stripped to her slip because of the heat, Carla flicked through the pages of last month's *World of Fashion*.

"I need to work on my suntan, with a nice shorts outfit. I've seen nothing that grabs me in the Department Store," she grouched. "Here, look. See what you think."

She gestured me closer, as if I was a normal human being, not a Stripey. I leaned over her smooth, soap-smelling shoulder. Together we stared at happy girls posing in swimsuits and beach wraps. "Something like that spotted one on the right?" Carla suggested.

"But nicer," I replied.

"I'll be the pride of the poolside."

"There's a *swimming pool* at Birchwood?" The words blurted out before I could stop them.

"Not for Your Sort," Carla huffed. "Just for proper people."

She pulled a silver cigarette case out of her jacket pocket and opened it with a flick, as if she were a starlet in a casino. There were five cigarettes in the case. I stared at them, still stunned by her casual words. *Not for Your Sort.*

I was standing right next to her, breathing the same air,

sweating in the same heat. Swap our clothes, and then what would we be?

But we were at Birchwood. Carla was a human being. I wasn't anymore.

Once you were on a List you weren't a person. Usually it meant you'd end up dead not long after, or at Birchwood, which was more or less the same thing.

Carla shook the cigarette case at me. The gesture was obvious — *take one.*

What would Rose do?
Ignore Carla's thoughtless generosity.

What would Marta do?
Stay alive.

I took all five cigarettes.

Mostly the guards stood in the shade during the most sweltering roll calls, leaving the prisoner bosses to go up and down the ranks, counting. Hours could pass if the tally wasn't right. Meanwhile we fried in the full sun like eggs in a pan.

Every day Rose stood by me. Her eyes would be fixed on some invisible spot far away. Me, I daydreamed I was eating tubs of lemon sorbet . . . buckets of lemon sorbet . . . I was *bathing* in lemon sorbet. Anything to avoid noticing what was going on all around: not to see, not to hear, not to smell.

One morning, running from roll call to the workshop, I noticed that Rose's head was bare. Bad enough that she put up with those clownish mismatched shoes; going bare-headed was madness.

I grabbed her arm and stopped running.

"Your headscarf! You've lost it! Rose, you can't keep losing things!"

Honestly, she was *hopeless*. She had already lost her spoon. We were given one bowl and one spoon each. Without them you couldn't eat. Rose had to drink soup straight from her bowl. She said she didn't mind.

"Saves on the washing up," she'd joked, as if there was anywhere to wash anything in the barrack block.

"I suppose you had nothing but silver spoons back at your palace?" I teased.

"*Such* a lot of work for the servants to polish," Rose agreed. "We actually had a special piece of cutlery just for eating pineapples. They were the housekeeper's pride. I love pineapple, don't you? So hard and prickly on the outside, but inside — oh, the soft yellow flesh and the juice . . . It was like drinking happiness."

I licked my cracked lips. I'd never had pineapple juice in my life.

"But where's your headscarf? Did you let someone steal it?"

"No! There was a woman at roll call — didn't you see her, standing in front of us?"

"I didn't see anyone. . . . Oh, the one who fainted?"

I vaguely remembered a little commotion as the woman's bones folded and she'd crouched on the ground like a crab until hauled to her feet again. "The old woman?"

"I gave it to her."

"Have you got sunstroke or something? Because if you haven't now, you soon will. That was *your* headscarf. Why'd you give it away?"

"She needed it."

"So do you! Marta will kill you for not being dressed properly. Who was the old bag anyway?"

Rose shrugged — a little squirrel shoulder hunch. "I don't know. Somebody. Nobody. She just looked so sad and so alone. Her eyes — lost — you know? She was shaking when I knotted the headscarf on. She couldn't even manage to say thank you."

"How ungrateful is that?"

Rose shook her head. "More like she'd forgotten there was anything to say thank you for. She wasn't that old either. She could have been my mother — or yours. Ella, wouldn't you like to think somebody somewhere was looking after them?"

That shut me up.

We never saw the crab-woman again.

Inside the sewing room the world shrank to a set of stitches. I curled over my work so only the knobbles of my spine showed — I was so skinny I could practically feel them grazing the rough fabric of my striped dress. Needle in, needle out, thread pulling. This was how I would survive till the end of the War. Then I would start my dress shop and never see ugly things again.

We'd opened the windows in the workshops once, just once, in early summer, in the hope that some air would crawl inside. Our hands were damp, the fabrics were limp, and the sewing machines almost burned to the touch when the sun was highest. The guard at the far end of the room had sweat patches on her uniform.

Froggy Francine went to the windows. They were high up so people couldn't really see in or out. The window frames were warped from the heat. Francine banged at one with the heel of her hand. It flew open. The others were even more stubborn. Finally there were squares of open sky.

As if under a spell, all the girls in the sewing room turned their heads, closed their eyes, and opened their mouths.

"Makes me want to run along and pop buttons in," Rose murmured.

With the windows open, we'd all waited for a freshness that never came. Instead there was dust. After days without rain, Birchwood mud had dried, cracked, and crumbled to a fine yellow-brown powder, which the lightest breeze blew around in little corkscrews. Now it came trickling over the windowsill.

"You'd better close them up again," I told Francine. "We can't get dirt on the clothes. You know that."

"I don't give a monkey's arse about the clothes," Francine muttered. "I need to *breathe*." She drew herself up tall.

She was still short. She glared at me. I glared back. My fists clenched.

There was a sudden burst of dog barking and bullets banging outside. Francine flinched . . . and closed the windows.

I hated the moment when we had to hand back our tools — *Pins!* called Marta — fold our work, and go outside to join the zebra herds in un-beautiful Birchwood.

The camp was all straight lines. Rows and rows and rows of barrack blocks stretching out as far as the eye could see. Where they ended, the barbed wire began. Between the buildings Stripeys stumbled, sat, stretched out in exhaustion. Some of them were like ghost-women. Their bodies were the embers of a fire that was dying out.

After work I dragged Rose through the crowds to get the best place in the soup line. Too near the front and we'd just be served salty water. Too near the end and there'd be burnt scrapings from the bottom of the pot or, worse, nothing. Somewhere in the middle was best. Then you might even get a piece of potato peeling.

My grandma made soup so thick you could practically stand a spoon up in it. One time Grandad actually took his knife and fork and pretended to cut it up.

I hoped Grandad was getting the groceries in and making sure Grandma was fed all right. She hadn't been so strong back in spring. She was probably better now. Nothing kept her out of action for long. Eventually Grandad would get sick of scratching together his own meals and he'd nudge Grandma out of bed and into the kitchen. She'd slap him with a spatula a couple of times, call him an old fool, then get back to the business of being up and about.

Life's too short to waste time being sick, she always said.

One day there was no supper at all. We got such measly portions at each meal, you'd think missing one wouldn't matter, but it was agony. I was almost tempted to chew on thread just to have something in my mouth.

That afternoon, I had a blistering headache from squinting too much. I was sewing teeny tucks on a set of lingerie for one of the officers' wives. Rose had burned her hand on the iron, and there was no cream for it, so she was subdued too. I would've preferred it if she'd cried or complained. Being Rose, she just carried on, pretending she was fine.

At least she had a new headscarf—two of Carla's cigarettes had seen to that. The cigarettes came out of my stash, from the little cloth pocket-bag I'd cobbled together, hidden inside my dress. It was fair payment for the embroidery Rose had done.

We were all packed up and ready to quit the workshop when a guard suddenly marched in and shouted, "Sit! Nobody leaves."

"We'll miss supper!" I dared to object. There were murmurs of support from the others.

"So you don't eat!" Marta butted in, glaring. "You were told to *sit.* You—Princess—get away from the window!"

63

Rose was on tiptoes trying to peek out. Her face was pale.

"They're moving people from the train platform," she said. "More than usual."

I shuddered. I didn't want to be reminded of the station where trains from all across the continent terminated . . . where lovely real life terminated. *Platform* to me now meant a place of dogs and screams and guards and suitcases. Men torn from women, women torn from babies, me being jostled along helplessly like a leaf in a dirty river.

At the train platform we'd been sorted to right or left. Work or chimneys. Life or death.

"Exactly," said Marta. "It's chaos out there. I don't want any of my workers getting caught up and accidentally . . . going to the wrong place."

The guard nodded and left the workshop, closing and locking the door behind her.

Now we heard it—the dull *tramp, tramp, tramp* of people walking. Hundreds, thousands of feet shuffling in the dust.

From what I heard, there were ten thousand people a day arriving on their one-way trip that summer. *Ten thousand a day.* That was surely more people than lived in my whole town. That number, arriving every single day.

Some stayed in the camp. The rest . . . I sewed extra quickly, as if each inch stitched me more firmly to life.

The problem was, Birchwood was bursting at the seams. There were three, even four of us to a mattress now. One blanket between two. Not enough jobs to go around. Day and night the trains kept arriving. The locomotive whistles kept shrieking. They reminded me of my own journey across unseen landscapes to reach Birchwood. Days and nights of jolting along train tracks. Waiting. Wondering.

In the evenings, scared new Stripeys came crowding into the barrack blocks, blinking and crying. They came from every corner of the continent, babbling in every language, showing just how far fighting had spread from the iron-hard homeland at the War's center. Somehow we all made ourselves understood.

Were we winning the War? Depended who you asked. The guards were always bragging about new conquests, new victories.

In the meantime, every new Stripey was given their number and their badge—red triangles, green triangles, and enough yellow stars like mine to make a galaxy of constellations.

My town was hundreds and hundreds of miles away to the northeast. The prisoners talked about cities that smelled of spiced pepper stew, or southern islands that baked blue and white in summer sunshine. There were Stripeys from as far west as you could go without falling in the ocean—Shona's countrywomen. They were marvelously haughty, so elegant somehow. I could imagine making dresses for them after the War. Stripeys from eastern lands were more solid, like Francine. Good workers.

Whatever their race or place, all the incomers were pounced on for news of the real world—*Where are you*

from? How's the War going? When will the liberators come?
Some of us fed on the rumors that there were still some
countries free to fight back. Our liberators, we hoped.

That was all very well. I preferred to ask how fashions
were changing. Were hems longer or shorter? Sleeves puffed
or flat? Skirts pleated or straight? I spent ages concocting
dresses in my head while Rose wandered off with some
lumpy woman from her own part of the world—a place
of fields, forests, music, and beauty, as far as I could tell
from Rose's descriptions. You never knew with Rose what
was real and what was a story.

We were overcrowded as an anthill, but still the people
kept coming. Call me a custard-yellow coward, but that hot
summer's evening, I couldn't bear to listen to that *tramp,
tramp, tramp* of feet outside the sewing room.

Tramp, tramp, tramp. On it went. A murmur of voices.
Babies crying.

Shona jumped when she heard the children. Beautiful,
graceful Shona, all legs and eyelashes—the giraffe. She'd
only been married a year when They came to arrest her
because her name was on a List. Her husband and baby
had been on the List too. She sometimes sang soft lullabies
to her sewing machine. The guard at the back of the room
occasionally caught a note and hummed the lullabies too . . .
then she'd stride forward and slap Shona's head to get her to
shut up. That night, Shona's eyelashes were wet with tears.

"My baby," she wept. "My precious little baby!"

66

Marta whirled around. "Who said that?"

Shona choked on her tears. Rose suddenly spoke up, "Did you ever hear the story about the queen and the lemon-curd tarts?"

Such a ridiculous, funny, perfect thing to blurt out! It was as if someone had sprinkled cool water on us. Everyone turned to look at Rose, perched on the edge of a table with her squirrel eyes sparkling.

Rose waited.

Marta nodded — *Go on* . . .

I already knew this about Rose — that just when you felt like snarling at the whole world, she'd start spinning some story about a girl who frowned and the wind changed and her face stayed like that. Or about an ogre who shouted so loudly it knocked the moon out of the sky.

It had started one bedtime back in the barrack. We had an extra Stripey jammed into the bunk with us, so Rose and I snuggled close.

"I miss books *so* much," Rose had said, sighing. "Sometimes my mother used to read to me, if she wasn't busy writing. I read under the bedcovers too, with a flashlight. Stories are much more exciting that way. How about you? What's your favorite book of all time?"

That stumped me. "We never really had books much. Grandad reads the newspaper — mostly for the crossword and the cartoons. Grandma has *Fashion Forecast*, obviously."

"You don't have *books*?" Rose almost sat up and banged

her head on the roof rafters. That made the rats jump. "How can you *live* without reading?"

"Pretty well so far." I laughed. "Stories are just made-up stuff anyway."

"Says who? I think they're a different way of telling the truth." Then, "Seriously — no books? Oh, Ella, you have no idea what you've been missing! Stories are food and drink and life. . . . I mean, haven't you even heard the story about a girl who made a gown out of starlight?"

"A gown out of starlight? How could you even do that?"

"Well," said Rose. "Once upon a time . . ."

And that was that. No sleep for me till Rose wrapped up with a triumphant *The end*.

Rose never ran out of tales to tell. She wove stories out of nothing, like a silkworm spinning a cocoon, or a fairy-tale maiden turning straw into gold.

Did I ever tell you about the time . . . ? was her opening line. What followed would be amazing cascades of complete nonsense. Things like her life as a countess in a palace with egg cups plated in real gold. In Rose's stories, people danced until dawn under the light of a hundred chandeliers, then slept in beds as big as boats, under silk quilts stuffed with downy feathers. The palace had walls made of books, and spires that touched the moon when it hung low in the sky.

"And unicorns roaming the park, and fountains spouting

fizzy lemonade, I suppose?" I teased her after that particular yarn.

Rose had looked grave. "Now you're just being silly," she said.

While we were trapped in the sewing room, Rose kept her story going for three whole hours. Outside there was the steady beat of shoes, boots, and sandals: *tramp, tramp, tramp.* Inside we were lost in a world where queens baked tarts and lemon trees talked. There were ogres who came and took the queen, even as her hands were covered in flour. The lemon-curd tarts tasted of sunshine and tears, and they had all the queen's rings hidden inside, where the ogres wouldn't find them. There was a princess who hid in a tree so the ogres didn't find her at first, either, until they sniffed her out and carried her off to their lair, which was a dismal place without trees or grass.

"Sounds like here," muttered Francine.

At another point, Francine laughed so hard she was shaking and crying, "Stop, *stop,* or I'll pee myself!" Later on, Marta hid her smile behind her hand. It was the first time I'd seen Marta being as human as the rest of us. Even the guard at the far end of the room listened in and smirked at the funny bits.

It came as a shock when Rose suddenly finished the story with a flourish: "And *that* was the end of *that.*"

"No, no, no!" everyone protested.

"Shh," said Shona. "Listen."

* * *

Silence.

The guard went to the workroom door and opened it a sliver.

"All clear!" she shouted. "Go on—get out—go!"

We ran to roll call. We had to dodge the debris dropped by those marching, marching incomers. There a handkerchief, yellow with snot. There a canary-colored feather blown out of a hat. And there, already sprinkled in dust, a single shoe for a baby's tiny foot.

That night, as we stood in our rows of five to be counted, there were no stars, no moon, no sky. Birchwood was buried in smoke. I tasted ash and for once felt no hunger.

"Rose?" I asked in the dark. The barrack that night was airless and even more crowded than usual. The straw we slept on seemed extra hot and scratchy. "Rosalind? Are you awake?"

"No," she whispered back. "Are you?"

"*Shh!*" hissed the bag of bones lying on my other side.

Rose and I huddled together so our words didn't have to go far from lip to ear.

"Your story was good today," I murmured. "You should be a writer."

"My mama is," said Rose. "A really good one. That's why my family got arrested—she wasn't afraid to publish books that told the truth, instead of what They want us to believe."

There was no chance to ask about the arrest. Rose was tumbling on into the next sentence.

70

"I'd love to be even half as good at writing as her. How about you?"

"Me? Write! That's a laugh. I sew."

"No, how about your mother, I meant."

"Oh, nothing much to say about her."

"There must be," said Rose.

Truth was, I couldn't really remember much about my mama. "She had to go back to work when I was just a baby. She was at a big factory, sewing suits. Nobody talks about it, but I think my father must've been one of the factory managers or something. They weren't married. Can you believe they had machines that could cut through twenty double layers of suiting wool at once?"

"Your mother, Ella?" Rose prodded gently.

"Grandma brought me up, really. The suit factory moved to another town, and all the workers had to go with it or lose their jobs. Mama visited every few weeks. Then every few months. Then she just sent money. Then the War happened, the factory made uniforms, and she didn't get paid. And then . . . you know." I shrugged in the dark.

Mothers weren't something I knew much about.

Two thin arms circled me in a hug.

"What's that for?" I grouched.

Rose gave me a squeeze. "Just measuring to see how far around my arms will go."

Later that night a woman somewhere on the bottom row of bunks began to sob, quietly at first, then uncontrollably.

"Why me, why me, why me?" she was wailing. "What have I ever done to be suffering here?"

"Shut up!" Girder bellowed from her private cubicle at the end of the block.

"I won't shut up!" the woman shrieked. "I want to go home! I want my husband and my babies! Why did They come for us? What had we done?"

"I said, *shut it!*" Girder roared.

The woman was too far gone. She screamed and screamed and screamed until I thought my ears would split. In the dark, Rose reached out a hand and found mine.

Girder exploded into action. She dragged the woman from the bunk and shook her. "It's not you!" she shouted. "It's nothing to do with you. It's Them. They want someone to hate. To kill. So They decided we're all criminals."

"I'm not!" said Rose abruptly, in a tone of great indignation.

"Me either!" cackled a rough girl from two bunks away. She had a green triangle badge; she was well known to have a criminal record longer than a roll of toilet paper.

"I used to steal apples," came a creaky voice from near the floor. "Sour as vinegar, and made your tummy twist inside out, but every autumn we nicked 'em all the same."

Girder folded her arms. "You stupid idiots. They don't care if you shoplifted lipstick, or even if you mugged an old lady for her pension money . . . or hacked your mother to death for that matter. Whatever we might've done, we're not here for *real* crimes."

The barrack went deadly quiet. Not even a stalk of straw rustled.

Girder liked having an audience. "Haven't you thick turds noticed They don't care what we've done? We're here because we're not *people* to Them. Even us green-triangle criminals, that's just an excuse. And you, red-triangle Rosy posy, with your manners and etiquette and all that crap — d'you think They'd sit down and have tea with you? It'd be like asking a rat to show you which feckin fork you need for the fish course!"

"How very rude," said Rose, though whether she was referring to Girder's bad language or the thought of dining with a rat, I couldn't tell.

"Rude?" Girder spat the word out. "It'll be the death of us!"

"They don't want all of us dead," I objected.

"Nah, not so long as we're useful, little sewing girl. But what about when they've had enough of playing dressy-up? You think it'll be all, *Ooh, I'm loving this little silk number* then? You'll be crispy-bones up the chimneys, same as the rest of us."

"Shut up!" I shouted straightaway, putting my hands over my ears. *"Shut up, shut up, shut up about chimneys."*

Next thing I knew, Girder was dragging *me* down from the bunk, every bone banging against the wood. I'd barely found my feet before she punched me in the mouth, yelling, *"I'm* the boss. *I'm* the only one who shuts people up in here — get it?"

She let go. I crumpled to the floor like a discarded rag. Girder looked down at me and sighed. Anger seemed to drain out of her, like pee leaking from the toilet bucket in the corner.

I was trembling as she helped me to my feet and pushed me back up to the top bunk. She turned to the woman who'd started off the whole rant.

"I want to go home!" the poor woman gasped, in between shakes and sobs.

"And I want to murder every last beast in this hellhole with my bare hands," Girder raged. She had hands as big as dinner plates. "The best we can do is *live*. Are you listening? The only way to beat them is by not dying. So shut up and survive, you miserable cow. And let the rest of us *sleep*."

I began to forget there'd ever been a world other than Birchwood. A world where people could travel by trains to proper destinations, such as places with shops, or the seaside. Where you could wear normal clothes and sleep in your own bed, and sit down to dinner with your family. You know — real life.

Rose said stories were life. I knew better. Work was life. Whatever Marta told me to do, I said, "I can do it." However tight the deadline, however fussy the client, I never ever let her down. In return I was getting the best jobs. The extra bread. The cigarettes and the occasional *well done*.

I was learning a lot, sometimes just by looking, sometimes

when I got help with a garment. The other seamstresses weren't as unfriendly as I'd first thought. They didn't begrudge sharing skills and knowledge. Bit by bit I found out their stories too. Real-life stories, from before Birchwood.

Francine, for example, had been in a big industrial workshop before coming here. I'd thought that already, having seen her power through heavy jobs. For Francine it was a whole different kettle of fish to sit in a small room sewing different things every week. She didn't get used to the toilet facilities, though. She kept badgering me for more "bog roll," as she called it.

Shona was once the star seamstress at a wedding-dress emporium. She told us all sorts of tales about obnoxious brides and their monstrous mothers. "Satisfying both at once was impossible," she said. "When you *finally* made the bride happy . . . that was *almost* worth the aggravation."

Shona was always touching her finger, where a wedding ring would have been. They'd taken all jewelry when we arrived. I'd only had the little yellow-gold locket Grandad had given me for my last birthday. It had my name inside and my birth date.

"Did you make your own wedding dress?" I asked Shona.

Shona smiled. "I did. Just a day dress in caramel crêpe fabric. When I got big with baby I cut it into a romper suit for him." Her face crumpled.

By midsummer I had my own sewing machine that no one else could use. I was even trusted with pins —*pins!*

When Marta was busy in the fitting room, I became boss of the workroom. The other seamstresses had to obey me. I managed to get Rose doing embroidery instead of ironing and cleaning all the time. Rose wasn't exactly grateful.

"Come on," I said. "We're almost like prominents now. You're the best embroiderer here: you deserve a promotion. Those dandelions you did on that nightgown the other day, they were so pretty."

"I like dandelions," Rose said. "Except when I first came here and my job was picking dandelions and nettles to make into soup. I had more blisters than skin from that. Anyway, we used to have a meadow of dandelions on the palace grounds, and buttercups, too. Do you know that thing with buttercups, where you hold them under your chin to see if you like butter or not?"

"What? Everyone likes butter. My grandma made the best bread-and-butter pudding, with really creamy milk, and . . . and that's not the point! Stop distracting me from work. Carla's after a new summer blouse with daisies embroidered on the collar, for starters. She'll give me cigarettes if it's nice. I could organize you a proper pair of shoes instead of those daft ones you've got now."

Rose looked down at her satin slipper and her leather brogue.

"I've become rather used to them," she said. "One makes me feel like a dainty lady, and the other is all about marking off the miles. There's a story in that."

"How can you keep turning everything into stories?"

"And how can you keep accepting gifts from a *guard*?"

"She's a *client*," I corrected her, though Carla usually came to her fittings in full uniform, complete with whip. Sometimes she even brought Pippa, tying the leash around the leg of the chair. Pippa would lie down and watch my every move with her yellow teeth showing. Dogs here were trained to attack Stripeys.

"Come on, Rose. Don't look at me like that! Carla's friendly in her own stupid way. Like a big sow that rolls around squashing her own piglets."

Rose smiled and tucked her arm through mine. I let her. We were outside lining up for evening coffee-water and it was safer to be two than one.

"Do you always compare people to animals?" she asked. "You've got a whole zoo by now—Carla the pig, Francine the frog, and Marta the shark."

"Don't tell them that's what I call them!"

"Of course I won't. So what about me? What animal am I, then?"

"Never mind."

"What animal?"

"A squirrel."

"A *squirrel*?" she shrieked. "Is that how you think of me? All skittish and scared?"

"Squirrels are cute! They have nice fluffy tails, and that way of tipping their head on one side when they look at you. I *like* squirrels. Why, what sort of animal do you want to be? A swan, I suppose. Something grand like that, fitting for a *countess* who lived in a palace with gold egg cups?"

"Swans have got a good hard *bite.*" Rose laughed, pecking me with her hand.

I fought her off, wriggling and giggling. "Stop it, you idiot!" It was really annoying how she kept making me happy. I was supposed to be concentrating on other things — like getting ahead and getting home.

People in the coffee-water line looked at us as if we were mad.

"Tell me — what sort of animal are you, then?" Rose challenged me.

"I don't know! Nothing. Or something stupid. Never mind." *Snake, piranha, spider, scorpion.*

Rose did that squirrel-tilt thing with her head. "I think I know what animal you are."

I didn't dare ask.

Day after day sewing. Night after night talking, then sleeping and dreaming.

Dreams of home. Of the table set for breakfast, with a clean cotton cloth. Fresh toast slathered in proper yellow butter. Eggs with bright yolks. Tea from a pot painted with yellow polka dots.

I always woke up before I got to eat anything.

* * *

A runner came to the barrack block one evening after roll call. She was a teeny little Stripey, like a bird. A starling, perhaps. She spoke to Girder. Girder called my number. I climbed down from the top bunk, trying to hide my fear. It couldn't mean anything good.

"See you soon," Rose called brightly, as if I was just popping out to pick up a pint of milk.

Off I went with the Starling, running of course. Down the main street. Past row after row after row of barrack blocks. To a cobbled yard and a big building with glass in the windows and strips of material that looked suspiciously like curtains. To a door.

Starling put her finger to her lips. *You first*, she mimed. *Stuff that*, I mimed back.

Starling sighed and pushed the door open. I paused before following, as if I had a choice in the matter. I was nearly piddling myself with nerves (quite an achievement when all summer I'd been sweating more than I drank, so it was hard to pee at all).

Inside, rows of closed doors. The smell of lemon disinfectant. The murmur of muted voices. At one door, a pair of boots. The Starling tapped on a blank door . . . then vanished so quickly I almost suspected her of flying away like a real bird.

The door opened.

"Don't just stand there, quick, come in — shut the door behind you. Wipe your feet. Take a seat. What do you think? It's not much, but it's home."

I was in the guards' barracks. I was in Carla's room.

* * *

Carla looked cool and fresh in the yellow sundress I'd made for her. She pointed her toes like a ballet dancer so I could admire her slippers.

"Aren't these sweet? One of the girls spotted them at the Department Store and I knew they'd do for me. Just my size, too, luckily."

One of the girls—another guard.

Carla laughed nervously. "Don't worry, it's all right: I won't get into trouble having you here, as long as we keep our voices down and nobody sees you. Sit on the chair if you like; let me just take the cushion off. Or on my bed. This bed, not that one—that's Grazyna's. She's on duty at the moment. You've probably seen her around. She's got really frizzy hair—looks a fright. It's all the swimming she does. I tell her she'll get too muscly, but she doesn't listen."

I'd seen Grazyna at work. Grazyna carried a well-worn wooden truncheon. This wasn't the right time to tell Carla we Stripeys called her Bone-Grinder, after an ogre who featured heavily in one of Rose's stories.

Carla sat on the bed. The mattress springs boinged. I took the chair. She patted the patchwork quilt spread over the bed, all browns and beiges.

"I thought you'd like this. See—it's stitched from pieces of dress leftovers, all different sorts."

It looked like a mishmash of my grandad's least-favorite ties. My grandma had a much nicer quilt on her bed back home, with cheerful flower prints and stripes. It was like a storybook of our lives. Grandma would say, *Do you remember having a frock made of this when we went for a picnic by the river and ate custard tart with nutmeg on top? Do you remember your grandad's old waistcoat, the one he wore to work, usually with the buttons done up wrong? Do you remember . . . ? Do you remember . . . ?*

The bed boinged again as Carla leaned forward. I could see speckles of face powder on her cheeks. "What's the matter? Are you OK?"

I nodded. Then I nearly jumped out of my skin as Carla thrust her wrist under my nose.

"Smell this! It's Blue Evening perfume. Look, here's the bottle." Up she sprang, going to a chest of drawers covered with cards and photographs. She picked up a blue cut-glass bottle with a starry metal cap. "I read somewhere that the most glamorous women spray a mist of perfume into the air then walk right through it. Try some!"

I held out my wrist cautiously.

"God, you're skinny! I wish I could diet more. I suppose I'm just stuck with these curves," she said.

Drops of Blue Evening frosted my skin. I smelled sharp sophistication and soft fur wraps. Chilled drinks in fragile glasses. High heels and shimmering silk. After these first brash top notes came a more subtle aroma. Flower petals, slowly falling. I thought of a storybook place Rose called the City of Light, full of sparkle and style. After the War, me and her, we'd wear perfume every day to drive out the stink of Birchwood. But not this scent. It was so strong in Carla's little room it made me want to gag, like a cat coughing up a hairball.

"So . . . can't you guess?" Carla demanded.

Guess what?

She twirled around in the middle of the room. "It's my *birthday*! I've even had my hair done specially. The hair salon here is *wonderful*. I'm nineteen today—practically middle-aged! Look, the cards are from Mama and Papa and my little brother Paul, and my old gym teacher—what a dragon!—and Frank, this boy in the village, but I didn't like him as much as he liked me. And that one's from Aunty Fern and Uncle Os, who've got the farm next to ours. They're the ones who sent the cake. Aren't you just gagging for a slice? I know I am. Do you like chocolate? It's chocolate sponge with chocolate buttercream in the middle and chocolate icing on top. I've even got candles."

Carla lit the candles, puckered up her lips (glossed red for the occasion) and blew the candles out.

"There! I made a wish!"

Good for you, I thought. I had a few wishes stored up of my own. *I wish I could go home. I wish I could be the most celebrated dressmaker in all the world*, and, most urgently, *I wish she'd just get on and cut the cake.*

That last wish came true pretty quickly. Carla passed me a big, brown slab of wonderfulness, with buttercream oozing out.

"You don't mind fingers, do you?" she asked. "There's only

us, and they don't exactly go for cake forks in this place, do they? Ha, ha."

I tried a small nibble. *Sugar!* My taste buds threatened to explode with shock and delight.

"I had presents too," Carla announced with her mouth full. "Don't look so guilty: I didn't expect *you* to get me anything. Anyway, I got a new hairbrush and comb set from Mama and Papa. I told them I didn't need one as there are *tons* for free at the Department Store. They sent these too—ha! I knew you'd like them. *World of Fashion*, every issue for the past three months, complete with paper patterns for a summer bathing suit and beach wrap, and all sorts . . ."

Carla spread the magazines on the bed and began turning the pages one by one. In her faux-posh farm-girl accent she began a running commentary: *Isn't it divine. . . . God, that's hideous. . . . I LOVE this one. . . . No one in their right mind would wear THAT in public!*

I felt sick. It was the sugar . . . the perfume . . . her *voice*, going on and on and on. Puking onto the patchwork quilt would be bad.

Carla pointed a sticky finger to one of the magazine designs. "You can make this for me. What do you think— too flashy? Too showy? I thought, with autumn not far off, it'd go well with a little knitted jacket from the Department Store. You know, I never realized Your Sort could sew so well. After the War I'll open a dress shop. I'll design and model the clothes and you can make them."

I nearly choked at the idea.

Carla veered off to the next monologue, this time fetching a picture from the chest of drawers.

"See this photo — this is me and Rudi, one of the farm dogs back home. Isn't he adorable? I couldn't bring him with me. Never mind, I've got Pippa now. A girl's best friend is her dog, right? This field where me and Rudi are, it's all buttercups and daisies this time of year — yellow from hedge to hedge. Did you ever do that thing with daisies where you pull the petals off to see if someone loves you? Loves me . . . loves me not . . ."

She was so close I could see clots of mascara on her eyelashes. I thought of Pippa, who looked more likely to pull people's heads off than petals. I put my plate down.

"You're not going, are you? So soon? Here, I'll wrap more cake in a napkin for you to take. *I* can't eat it all — not and still fit into this dress, ha, ha. The other girls aren't getting any. They're not really *friends*, you know, not even Grazyna. They don't have an eye for fashion and nice things like me. You understand. I know you do. . . ."

I made it to the door.

"Yes, hurry before anyone sees you," said Carla, suddenly anxious. "Go!"

The whole time I hadn't spoken a single word.

Back at the barrack Rose and I curled into a secret circle on our bunk. The remains of the cake slice lay splodged on a napkin between us. It was a thing of wonder.

"It doesn't seem possible that cake and Birchwood can exist together in the same place," Rose said.

"I know! It's crazy. What on earth made Carla invite me to her *birthday?* Some sort of sick joke? Then offering me *cake!*"

"She's trying to be friends with you. She's wrong to abuse you like that, but she does sound lonely."

"Lonely? You didn't hear her banging on about all her presents, and how she could get anything she wanted at the Department Store, and how the other guards *don't understand* her."

"Exactly. Lonely."

"Well, *boo-hoo* for her! The main thing is, we got cake out of it. Go on, it's for sharing. Not with everyone in the barrack," I added quickly, knowing how pathologically generous Rose was.

Rose touched the cake, then licked her finger with the tip of her tongue. She closed her eyes.

"Oh, how I've missed sweet things!"

I was mesmerized by how much Rose enjoyed the taste. She smiled and took a bigger scoop. She had a smudge of buttercream on her bottom lip. I wanted to lick it clean.

We weren't used to so much luxury. Stomach cramps caught up with us not long after. Well worth it.

The next day I washed the cake napkin out in the sewing-room sink, and Rose ironed it into a neat square. I spotted

Carla while I was running to evening roll call and thought I'd give her the napkin back. I got close enough to speak — close enough to set Pippa barking — but Carla marched straight past me, chin up, whip in hand. I was just one more nameless Stripey, not important enough to notice.

A few days later, when Marta stood in the center of the workshop and clapped her hands for our complete attention, we knew it had to mean something pretty monumental. Otherwise we'd never be allowed to stop working.

I looked for Rose. She smiled over at me from the ironing board, where she was gently pressing a panel of embroidered muslin. I smiled back. She mimed "accidentally" leaving the iron burning the fabric. My eyes widened in horror. Her eyes rolled. *Just joking.*

"Serious announcement!" Marta declared. "I've just had a meeting with none other than the commandant's wife. In person, at her house."

There were instant murmurs. The commandant and his family had a villa just on the outer prison wall. Sometimes Stripeys got to work there — a cushy job, I'd heard.

Marta was enjoying our curiosity.

"As you know, Madam likes to select the best gowns that come to Birchwood for us to alter and improve for her wardrobe. Now, someone very high-ranking will be visiting Birchwood soon, as part of an inspection. Madam will need a special dress. Nothing I could show her fits the bill, so she's told me to have something made here in the workshop. An evening gown, suitable for a woman of her standing . . ."

I didn't hear any more. I was already sketching that dress in my mind. A gown for a summer evening . . . not gaudy, not frivolous. Madam H. was a matron and a mother, after all. Yellow would do it. A mature yellow. A flowing satin in old gold or straw gold . . .

"Ella?"

I blinked. "Sorry. Yes?"

Marta frowned. "Didn't you hear me? I said I want you to take over Francine's work on that set of yellow pajamas so she's free to do the evening gown."

"Not likely!" I exploded. "I'm going to make the dress! Francine's work's *fine* if you want something plain and workaday — no offense, Francine . . ."

"Plenty taken," Francine retorted with a scowl.

I hurried on. "Sorry, it's just I've already got a gown in mind. The most amazing dress ever — sleeves to the elbows, very slight lift on the shoulder, darts under the bust, a wrap around the hips here, then satin cascading to the floor . . ."

I don't know how I dared go on and on like that. Maybe it was remembering one of Grandma's mottoes: *Shy kids get nothing.*

Francine and I stood facing each other like boxers in a ring. Except this was much more serious than that. Marta's eyes glinted as she watched us both. I suddenly realized that she'd set this up as a test, to see how far I was prepared to go to get ahead.

All the way.

Would I bad-mouth Francine's work? *Yes.* Hog the best machine and tools? *Yes.* Sabotage her sewing? *Maybe.* If I had to.

"Right," Marta said, with a cruel curl of her upper lip. "Let's see what you can both do."

"You won't regret choosing my dress," I said. "I can start right away. I need Madam's measurements, a mannequin, and five meters of yellow satin—not any old yellow, a very particular shade . . ."

I think Rose might have snorted at that point. Later, in the soup line, I asked why she was laughing.

"Just you being you," Rose answered with a grin. "Marta tells you to make a dress, and in your head it's already made. You really are a born designer, you know that?"

"Oh, Rose, you can laugh all you like, but it's going to be *gorgeous.* Best of all, I know how I want it decorated. I'll have a sunflower, embroidered in silk, right here on the bodice, so the happy petals reach out over the shoulder and across the sleeve seams. I'd like the threads all shaded, like an oil painting on the dress. We'll get beads for the seeds—hundreds of them clustered—"

"Whoa. Wait a minute, Miss Couturier! You're not serious, are you?"

"You don't think I'll be able to get the right shade of silk? You don't want to do embroidery with beadwork?"

"It's nothing to do with the silk or beads, it's about the whole wretched *dress*. Francine was picked first. Let her do it."

That stopped me short. The dream dress stopped floating in my imagination. It slumped to the floor in a limp pile.

"Why shouldn't I make it? Who knows what sort of reward I'll get? I'll be able to trade for better bunks in the barrack block, or even for a blanket each—wouldn't you like that?"

"Does a cat like cream? But that's not the point, Ella. Think who you're making the dress *for*."

"I know! The commandant's *wife*. She's the one who set up this workshop in the first place. She's got a really good eye for quality—nothing but the best—and when other officers' wives see her wearing *my* dress they'll *all* come flocking for their own fancy gowns."

Rose pulled away a little. "You really don't understand the problem, do you? You honestly don't see what's happening?"

"Success, *that's* what's happening. Don't try and talk me out of this, Rose. I've *got* to make this dress and I'm going to. End of story."

"Stories never have ends," said Rose, stubborn as a donkey. "There's always another chapter and a *what happens next*."

"What happens next," I snapped, "is that you stop poking your nose into my business! I *don't care* if I'm sewing for the commandant's wife! The only thing that matters is that I'm going to make the dress, whether you like it or not."

"I *don't* like it."

"You've made that perfectly clear."

"It's clear you've forgotten where you are and what happens here — and who makes it happen!"

"As if *you* know what's going on around you, with your head in la-la make-believe land!"

"You know what I see, Ella? I see all of us wobbling on this really fine line between staying alive and collaborating."

My mouth dropped open. "You're calling me a *collaborator*? That's an appalling thing to say! You're just jealous because you can't even organize proper shoes for yourself, let alone make dresses for other people! You'd be *nowhere* without me to get you extra bread!"

I was so angry I didn't know what to do with myself. We'd never argued like this before. It was Rose's fault for goading me.

She tried a different tactic. "Look, Ella, if it's more bread you want, share mine. I don't mind. Then you wouldn't miss the extra food from the sewing room."

God, she was so *exasperating*. She didn't understand *at all*. I would've stormed off there and then if it hadn't meant losing my precious place in the line.

Birchwood in summer meant days of scorching heat and nights of smoke. Stripeys wilted — so dry and thin they looked like paper dolls. Me, I was parched, I was famished, and I was sick from the taste of ashen air, but inside I made myself float above the dust, above the stink. I could've walked through barbed wire, electric fences, and speeding bullets without noticing. None of that was important, because, whether Rose liked it or not, *I was making the Dress!*

Most marvelously of all, Marta was letting me go shopping at the Department Store. As a peace offering, I volunteered Rose to come with me. She must still have been sulking or something, because she groaned when I told her.

"I *hate* shopping," she said.

"You have to come, Rose, *please*. Listen, I'm sorry you got cross before. Come with me to see this place. Think of it—a land of plenty!"

"I've *plenty* of work to do," Rose punned.

"Come on," I wheedled. "Marta's made a list about a mile long, and I can't carry everything."

"Ask Shona."

"She's sick today."

Shona was sick almost every day now. Instead of a graceful giraffe, she was more like a drooping daffodil, too long out of water. I think she was actually ill, rather than just pining for her husband and baby.

"Anyway," I said, "how can you hate shopping?"

"You've no idea how many fashion shows my mother dragged me to."

"You went to *fashion shows?*"

"Twice a year, for each new season's collections. Don't get me wrong—the clothes were unbelievable. I could've gobbled up every outfit, then gone back for seconds."

"You can't eat clothes."

"If only they were edible! I'm telling you, the fashions

91

in the City of Light were *delicious*. It was just the people who gave me indigestion. So many air kisses, so many *dahhhhhlings*, so many powdered faces and talon fingers. Nasty!"

"When I have my dress shop I'll charge extra to snooty clients like that."

"Ah, the famous Ella dress shop!"

"You wait, I'll do it. I'll be chauffeur-driven to all the best warehouses on proper fabric-buying trips . . ."

Rose tucked her arm into mine. "I'll do the driving if you let me wear a peaked cap. 'Step aboard, madam, and enjoy the ride.'"

"So you'll come to the Department Store with me?"

"Oh," I said. "I was hoping for something more . . ."

"Glamorous?" Rose mocked. "Revolving doors, vast glass windows, and pretentious potted plants?"

"Something like that."

The so-called land of plenty was, in fact, a series of about thirty huge huts, stretched across a section on the northern edge of Birchwood, not far from a cluster of parched birch trees.

We slipped through the nearest set of doors, not knowing what to expect.

The first building we came to was frantic with activity. It was called the Small Store. Guards and Stripeys all mingled together, choosing things from shelves or bustling around with parcels.

A woman named Mrs. Smith was in charge. Rumor had it she used to run a puff house. Rose asked me what that was. I pretended I knew but that it wasn't polite to tell her. Mrs. Smith was definitely one of the elite prominent prisoners.

She looked absolutely nothing like us normal Stripeys. She was elegant in a plain tailored suit of dark linen and simple heeled shoes. Her sparse hair looked as if it had been freshly shampooed and set. Her nails were painted. She was something like a cross between a hawk and a snake. A venomous snake.

She spotted us and her lips narrowed. I almost expected a forked tongue to come flicking out.

"Ah, Marta's girls from the workshop. Welcome."

There was as much warmth in Mrs. Smith's welcome as in an iceberg. Her voice wasn't cultured—not as posh as Rose's at any rate.

"The stores are rather overwhelmed at the moment, as you see," said Mrs. Snake. "At least ten thousand new packages each day. This much stock needs a lot of sorting, so my girls are always busy. I can just barely spare you an escort. Don't get ideas. Theft is *never* tolerated."

As she spoke, Mrs. Snake tapped her manicured fingernails against a row of crystal perfume bottles on the table in front of her. Carla's favorite, Blue Evening, was there. Out in the real world, each bottle would've cost more than my grandparents earned in a year. I ached to lift the stoppers and sniff the scents.

Mrs. Snake called to a short, round girl in a white blouse

and black skirt. "Take these two to the Big Store. Bring back a tally on nightgowns while you're at it; we've had a request for summer styles."

Our guide looked as if she'd never seen sunlight, she was so pale. She wore glasses with thick lenses, had very sloping shoulders and wide, white hands. When I saw her scurry to a pile of stuff to dig inside, I knew what sort of animal she'd be. A mole. Small, soft, and subterranean.

"They're prisoners, but they don't have to wear striped sacks," I whispered to Rose. "Aren't you just *aching* to get out of here and wear normal clothes again?"

Without once looking us in the eye, Mole scuttled out of the Small Store and into the Big Store—twenty-nine vast huts crammed with every kind of object ever owned. Suitcases, shoes, spectacles, soap, prams, toys, blankets, perfume . . . I saw one box filled with combs and brushes, some still with strands of hair clinging. My own shaved scalp prickled.

In between huts we saw Stripeys pushing carts with more and more cases, more and more bundles, all tied with thick string. Some strong-looking women in the outdoor sorting yards were even dressed in white shirts and black slacks, like normal people. There had to be a few thousand prisoners at work in this place—the strangest shop assistants you ever saw.

"Can you imagine being able to have whatever you want?" I said to Rose. "It's like a treasure trove."

94

"You mean an *ogre's* hoard," Rose replied contemptuously. "Stolen and stashed away."

"Hey, you could get yourself a better pair of shoes," I said. "I mean, an actual *pair*."

Rose shrugged. We followed Mole.

Each hut of the Big Store was like our barrack blocks with the same sort of wooden struts holding the roof up, but longer, wider, and higher. Mole brought us to one that made me wrinkle my nose. Birchwood was never fragrant, but this was a whole new world of smells. Damp. Mold. Sweat. Stinky feet. It made me feel sick. This wasn't what I'd had in mind at all.

An aisle down the middle of the hut was just wide enough for two people to pass, if they didn't mind a bit of a jostle. Every other inch of floor space was covered with stacks of suitcases and great lumpy mounds that reached back into the shadows and up to the rafters. Some of the piles were so high they threatened to topple over. I saw sleeves sticking out, and trouser legs, and bra straps, and odd socks.

"They're *clothes*," said Rose in the hushed tones usually saved for tiptoeing around religious places or art galleries, or for discussing anything to do with sex. "Mountains of clothes!"

Mole looked around and sighed. "Ten thousand suitcases a day. It's too much. We can't keep up. Every case is opened. All the contents sorted. Clothes, valuables, perishables.

Some of the food is moldy by the time we get to it, of course. Such a waste."

"Where do they all come from?" I blurted out. As soon as I'd said it, I wished I could reel the words back in. *Don't ask questions you don't want answers to, Ella.*

Mole looked at me as if I was missing a brain.

Rose glanced at me and quickly said, "What do you do with them once they're sorted?"

"What isn't kept in Birchwood gets fumigated then packaged up and sent by railway back to the towns. For victims of bombing raids, or just to be sold as secondhand goods," Mole said in a flat voice. "Every single garment has to be checked for valuables first. They hide money and jewelry in hems, in the seams, in shoulder pads, everywhere. Anything we find goes on these piles here in the center of the hut. The guards and bosses keep an eye out for anyone who thinks they might snag something for themselves. Yesterday they shot a girl who took a piece of jewelry. She said it was her mother's wedding ring. . . ."

Mole's voice trailed off for a moment. Then she resumed her description of Department Store sorting.

"All name tapes to be removed, and identifying marks. New owners don't need to know who once had their clothes. All dressmaker and tailor labels are snipped out carefully too and burned in the stove. Except for the most exclusive labels, of course. Couture clothes come to you girls at the sewing workshop."

I became hypnotized by the sight of Stripeys tugging

garments from a pile. Their hands moved like spiders over each item. *Snip* went the scissors if something was to be cut. *Clink* went coins poured into a tray. Money notes rustled. Gold twinkled. Slowly, reluctantly, clumsily, my mind was making the connection between the high-quality clothes we altered at the workshop and these suitcases spilling out all over the Department Store floors.

Ten thousand suitcases a day. Ten thousand people a day. All arriving, never leaving.

My heart beat faster. My focus went from the mountains of stuff to tiny details. Bobbles of fluff on a child's jumper. Sweat stains in the armpits of an old shirt. I saw cracked buttons, stocking holes, and darned vests.

There were fancier things too — satin bra straps and spangled skirts. My attention was caught by the shimmer of silk pajamas edged with swansdown and scented by stalks of lavender tied with a ribbon. These got set aside as special, along with diamanté-heeled shoes and a silver cigarette case. I saw nightgowns and ball gowns, swimsuits and evening suits, golf shoes and tennis shorts.

What sort of place did people think they were coming to?

As if anyone could imagine a place like Birchwood existed.

A thought began to uncurl in my mind: someone should get out of Birchwood to tell the rest of the world what was happening here. Other people on Lists had to know what was waiting for them at the end of the train line. My *grandma* had to be told: DON'T GET ON THAT TRAIN.

"Ella?"

Rose touched my hand. I broke out of my trance and trotted after her and Mole. My mouth tasted of vomit.

"Do you think . . ." I began, as we hurried on. "Do you think *our* things are in these piles? I don't like the idea of people rooting through my school satchel and reading my homework. I mean, what about our clothes, too? I had a beautiful sweater my grandma knitted. Is some other girl wearing it now? I bet she never stops to think who wore it first, or how it got to her."

Rose didn't answer.

I'd never asked Rose if she'd had time to pack. Whenever I tried to talk properly about her arrest she shrugged me off with fairy tales about being locked in a dungeon by ogres, then carried here by a wooden dragon and dropped into Birchwood with a bang.

We dodged around boxes stacked up to the rafters.

I'd heard most people were given a few minutes or even hours to pack their belongings for the train journey here. Me, I was just going down the street — in the gutter of course, because I was on a List and that meant I wasn't allowed to walk on the pavement — swinging my satchel, and wondering what would be in the new issue of *Fashion Forecast*. Next thing I knew, a truck with bars across the back windows pulled up next to me, and police were shouting and dragging me. I screamed for help. People in the street pretended not to notice. The truck doors banged shut, marking my very un-fairy-tale switch from one world to another.

I wondered, what would I have chosen to bring if I had had a chance to pack one suitcase? Clothes, of course, and soap and my sewing kit. *Food*, oh, all the food I could fit in a big bag!

"*Books*," breathed Rose, spotting a cascade of hardbacks.

What idiot would waste space lugging books when they could have clothes and grub? An idiot like Rose, obviously: she took a step forward, spellbound.

Mole caught her arm. "You can't have those. You came for fabric."

I fetched out the shopping list Marta had drawn up. Mole scanned it quickly. "Come this way."

In another hut, among the bolts and folds of fabric, I found exactly what I needed. I knew it would be perfect for Madam's dress. It was a heavy, fluid satin that shone like hazy sunshine on a too-hot field of wheat. It was in sections, rather than an uncut length. Nervously I smoothed the pieces out, checked them for size, and pulled a few stray threads from the edges. It was clearly the remains of another, bigger dress—a magical ball gown—unpicked for recycling. Who'd once worn it?

"What do you think, Rose? *Rose?*"

No sign of her.

* * *

I panicked. For one moment I imagined Rose buried under mounds of thousands and thousands of pieces of clothing. I had a vision of pulling at her arm, only to find it was an empty sleeve, or a trouser leg or . . .

Lost in contemplation of a book.

She wasn't even reading it. Someone else was — a guard.

He was a young guy with a bit of mustache fluff on his upper lip and a hand that kept dropping to hover over the gun on his belt. He'd obviously been at the book for a while. He was somewhere in the middle of it, tracing the words with a stubby finger. Rose's eyes were following that finger as if it was loaded with gold and diamond rings.

I hissed her name. Rose didn't hear me.

The guard didn't notice her standing there at first. When finally he did, his forehead crumpled with annoyance, but he just stared at her.

"Is it a good book?" Rose asked politely, as if he was some nice boy she'd bumped into at the local library.

The guard blinked. "Um, this? Yes. It's good. Really, really good."

"The sort you can't put down?"

"Um, yes."

Rose nodded. "I think so too. I'm biased. My mother wrote it."

The guard stared at her so hard I thought his eyeballs would actually pop out. A fiery blush crept up from his collar to the roots of his hair. He looked at Rose, then at the name on the spine of the book. Without another word, he closed the book, walked to the stove, and threw it in. The guard wiped his hands on his uniform as if they'd somehow been contaminated. If he could've scoured his eyes and purged his brain of that book, I think he would have.

I tiptoed over, turned a stone-cold, stunned Rose around, and guided her out of that hut.

"Hurry up!" said Mole. We both stumbled after her.

A room full of spectacles—thousands of glassy circles looking at nobody. A mountain range of shoes—brown brogues, football boots, dance sandals, ballet flats. New shoes, old shoes, dull shoes, bright shoes. Big shoes. Baby shoes.

My shoes . . . ?

Just clothes.

There was no hiding from the truth now. No looking away. No pretending. The Department Store wasn't a glorious treasure trove. It was a terrible graveyard of lives. We all came here wearing clothes and carrying luggage. Everything was tricked or ripped from us. Take away people's things, and you're left with a simple naked body that can be beaten or starved or enslaved or . . .

All those clothes and all that luggage could then be stored, sorted, cleaned, and reused. How horrifically efficient.

Rose had been right. This *was* an ogre's hoard, collected by modern, business-like ogres in suits and uniforms. Instead of a fairy-tale castle or dungeon, They had built a factory. It was a factory that processed people into ghosts and turned their possessions into profit.

Rose tripped over a small brown suitcase. It broke open and waves of photographs spilled out. Rose skidded and went flat down on her behind, surrounded by a sea of snapshots. Beach holidays. Baby cuddles. Wedding groups. First days at school.

Unknown eyes looked up at us as if to say, *Where are we? Why aren't we on the mantelpiece or by the bed or in the wallet anymore?* I helped Rose to her feet, conscious of all the faces being trampled. I heard Rose say "Sorry," as if they were real people. Which they once had been.

I clutched Rose and looked straight at her.

"We can't end up invisible or nonexistent," I gabbled. "We're still real, even if They've taken our clothes and shoes and books. We have to stay as *alive* as possible, as long as possible, just like Girder said. Do you know what I mean?"

Rose's gaze didn't waver. "We will live," she said.

I told myself, *Look down at your sewing, not up at the chimneys.*

I wrapped myself in a world of silk and stitching. I made the dress of dreams. Outside there were the sounds of trains and dogs, and the stink of latrines and worse. Inside there was me and the magic of my work. I had flashing scissor blades, a glittering needle, twinkling pins, and shimmering thread.

I set up a dressmaker's dummy, padded out to the exact shape of Madam's measurements. On the other side of the workroom, Francine did the same. I wasn't worried. Not after Francine picked out a cheap-looking chiffon fabric the color of baby vomit.

Rose did a lovely job of pressing my silk. I'd arranged with Marta for Rose to sew more, but she was still doing the ironing. Rose said she didn't mind ironing.

When she said that, Marta took me to one side and said, "What you don't understand about Rose is that she's not like us. We know what we have to do to survive. *She's* still stuck thinking she can be her own sweet self."

I wanted to say something to defend Rose. Nothing came out.

Marta nodded. "Rose wouldn't last five minutes without you. You'll be getting out of this place if you keep your head screwed on right. Her . . . I wouldn't bet on it."

Everyone in the workshop knew by now what a talented needleworker Rose was. Her fingers could turn skeins of silk into swans, stars, or flower gardens. She embroidered all the natural life we never saw in Birchwood — ladybugs, bees, and butterflies. She stitched yellow ducklings on a child's dress Shona was making for the daughter of a very high-up officer. The ducks looked so chirpy and so real you almost expected to see them waddle off the frock and into the nearest puddle of water. Except there wasn't any water in Birchwood, not for Stripeys, at any rate. Our lips were cracked with thirst. What came from the taps wasn't safe to drink.

When Shona saw those ducks, she just buried her face in the little frock and started to cry.

"Shh!" I said. "Marta's next door with a client. Don't let her hear you."

"I miss my baby," she sobbed.

"Course you do," said Francine. "We all miss somebody, isn't that right, girls? Now wipe your face and finish up that seam you're sewing."

"Look out!" said Rose.

The door to the fitting room opened. I saw Marta's fingers on the handle. She was chatting to a client.

"The child's dress? With the ducklings? Yes, sir, I'll just have it fetched for you. Yes, she will be growing fast at that age. . . . Just learning to talk, is she?"

Rose moved to hide Shona from Marta's view.

"Give me the dress, quickly," I hissed to Shona. "You know what'll happen if you're caught like this again."

"Give her the dress," said Francine.

"Come on, Shona," coaxed Rose.

Shona's cries grew louder and louder. I couldn't hold or quiet her.

What would Marta do?
Slap her.

104

* * *

I slapped Shona. Hard.

That happens in films when people get hysterical. I never thought it would actually work—not when getting slapped was all part of daily life in Birchwood. To my surprise, Shona drew in a deep breath . . . let it out . . . then slumped.

When Marta came back to the workshop, we were so quiet you could've heard a pin drop, if pin-dropping had been allowed. By then Shona was back at her machine, hemming curtains for the officers' quarters. The duck dress was, we heard later, a huge success with the little girl who got to wear it.

Rose was also working on the sunflower for *my* creation. She cut a sunflower shape in silk and backed it with a layer of batting and another layer of plain cotton canvas. With white tacking threads, she marked the lines that the sunflower petals and leaves would take. Next she unwound a length of silk from the skeins Marta had doled out, and she began to stitch. I loved watching Rose sew. She got so absorbed.

"I like embroidery," she said later, when we were curled up in our bunk together. "Sewing's when I come up with my best plots. My mother says she cooks up her stories in the kitchen, when she's baking. Tragedies turn the lemon cakes bitter. Comedies make her spicy dishes zing!"

"I thought you lived in a palace with an army of servants."

"Absolutely. Cook used to fume like a broody volcano

every time Mama took over the kitchen. You should've heard her bashing pots around and muttering, *It's not right, folk not knowing their proper place.* Mama didn't help matters. She was easily distracted and always left the washing up for someone else to do."

"For you?"

"Oh no! I've never washed a pot in my life, not till swilling out my soup-water dish here. My job was to listen to Mama's stories, lick the mixing bowl out, then eat whatever Mama had made."

"My grandma used to lie in the bath when she was inventing dresses, until the water went cold. The toilet was in the same room, so me and Grandad were always busting to go on days when Grandma was really inspired." I sighed. "Can you imagine ever getting to have a bath again?"

"Oh, yes," replied Rose quickly. "A massive soak, with bubbles piled up so high they spill over the edge. Along with a really good book and lots of fluffy towels."

"You *read* in the bath?"

"And you don't?"

"Do you like reading more than sewing?"

Rose hesitated. "Do I have to choose?"

"You do if you're going to come and work in my dress shop after the War."

"Ah, I've an invitation to join you in this place of wonder?"

I almost wriggled with joy at the thought of it. "Won't it be *amazing*? My very own shop. Perhaps some of the other

106

girls in the sewing room could join me. Shona's pretty good, and Hedgehog . . ."

"Who?"

"You know, the bristly girl who never smiles but sews a mean invisible hem."

"Oh, you mean Brigid? She can't smile."

"Why not?"

"The usual. She made a vow to the queen of the Frost Giants that she wouldn't smile for a year and a day."

"*What?*"

Rose sighed. "She's embarrassed about her bad teeth. A guard kicked her in the mouth once."

"Oh. Well, we need to find out if she wants a job when we get out of here."

"Any idea where this legendary dress shop will be?" Rose asked.

"Somewhere classy. A nice street — not too quiet, not too hectic. Big windows with ridiculously sumptuous displays, and a door with a bell that rings when customers arrive . . ."

"Thick carpets, bowls of happy flowers everywhere, and swags of curtains across the fitting-room cubicles?"

"Exactly!"

"Doesn't sound so bad, I suppose," Rose teased.

I stopped what I was doing, which was squishing the lice that lived in our dress seams.

"Not too bad? It will be the most wonderful thing *ever*!"

"Better than bread and margarine?"

"*Equal* to bread and margarine. Seriously, we'll wear smart suits and blouses with crisp white ruffles down the front. And put our hair up in the latest fashions . . ."

"Styled by the hairdresser next door."

"There's a hairdresser's next door?"

"Certainly."

"I was hoping there'd be a hat shop."

"There is," said Rose promptly. "Two doors along, next to a bookshop. And a bakery on our other side, run by a woman who specializes in iced buns and chocolate cream éclairs."

"Oh, god," came a voice from the bunk below. "Did someone mention chocolate?"

"Shhh!" said everyone else. "What if Girder hears?"

"Girder hears everything!" came the boss's big boom. "If there's chocolate anywhere in this block, it needs to reach me in no less than three seconds."

Rose continued in a whisper. "The place I have in mind is perfect for us. The streets aren't too busy. There's a park just opposite, with a fountain where the children go paddling in hot weather, and an ice-cream kiosk, and a magical apple tree that just snows blossoms in springtime."

Ice cream was almost too painful to recall. I loved creamy-yellow vanilla, with crystals of ice on the edge of the scoop, then the cold mouth-meltingness of it all . . .

"You make it sound so real," I said. "You and your storytelling!"

"Maybe it is real," Rose replied. "Maybe I know a place like that. Maybe it actually exists."

"Where is it, then? Anywhere near here?"

"Ha! As far from here as from the sun to the moon. It's in the most dazzling place in the world. A city full of art, of fashion . . ."

"And chocolate."

"Definitely chocolate. A city lit by so many lamps they actually call it the City of Light. *That's* where our shop will be, with our names scrolled in gold writing above the window — Rose and Ella."

"Ella and Rose," I corrected, gently but firmly.

The next day I was ready to savage something, someone, anyone.

"What's the matter?" Rose asked.

"Isn't it obvious? The dress is a complete disaster! I made the cotton toile as a practice piece and it seemed OK, so I cut the fabric and tacked it and it's totally *wrong*. The worst thing I've *ever* made."

A toile is a rehearsal — a dress rehearsal, if you like — where you put the dress together, but not in the actual fabric.

I groaned. "Francine will win, and Marta will have me sewing *cushions* if I'm lucky."

"Wrong how?" Rose asked.

"Just *wrong*."

"Ah. That explains everything."

"Don't make fun of me."

"Then tell me what needs doing to the dress to fix it. The size?"

"No, it's made to Madam's exact measurements."

"The draping?"

"No, that's fine. Except she probably won't like it."

"The color?"

I nearly exploded. "How can you *say* that? The color's *beautiful*. Look, stop trying to criticize it. Given the conditions I've been working in, it's a miracle I've done this well. Marta hasn't helped, always hovering, asking when it'll be ready."

"So it's good, then?"

(Why was she smiling at me?) "Not good enough."

"Of course it's good enough, and the next one will be better. That's how it works—you get experience and improve."

"Why can't I just be better *now*? This is the most important thing in the world to me, Rose. If I can't be a dressmaker, what am I? Nothing!"

Rose caught hold of me and hugged me close. "You're a good friend," she whispered in my ear. Then she kissed my cheek. The spot where she kissed me tingled for hours afterward.

Rose finished her sunflower while I was still wrestling with the dress. It had a burst of bright petals done in satin stitch, and knotted seeds so real-seeming I wanted to gouge them out and eat them.

"I know you had the flower in mind for the shoulder," she said, "but I think it would sit nicely on the hip, where the silk gathers and falls."

"No, it's got to be the shoulder." I held the flower there. Then switched it to the hip. Annoyingly, Rose was right. On the shoulder it looked tacky, on the hip it looked perfect.

Rose watched me. "Do you think it's nice enough?"

"Nice?" I nearly choked. "It's not nice. It's *wonderful.* The best embroidery I've ever seen."

How could she dismiss so much talent? At that moment I didn't know whether I wanted to shake her or . . .

My heart beat quickly and I bit my lip.

Or kiss her.

Then my machine was sabotaged.

I had my head down in pure concentration when a man came in. An actual male, opposite-gender *man.*

The effect was electric. The air crackled. Brigid touched her head, as if she still had hair to preen instead of hedgehog bristles. Francine pinched her cheeks to tease out a bit of color. Marta managed to look flustered too — probably because hormones were something even she couldn't boss around.

In Birchwood They mostly kept male and female Stripeys separate. The only men we saw on this side of the barbed wire were guards and officers. Now here was a male prisoner! A reminder of fathers, sons, brothers, husbands, and sweethearts. Not that *I'd* ever had a sweetheart.

Grandma would've turned inside out at the mere idea of a boy coming to call. *You're far too young to be thinking of that,* she would've said.

This was a young man — maybe a few years older than me. It was hard to tell in Birchwood, where all Stripeys seemed old. Somehow the usual blue-and-gray prisoner uniform looked clean and crisp on him. He carried a toolbox and had hands rough from manual work. If he was in one of Rose's fairy stories, he'd be the seventh son of a seventh son — poor but lucky, and destined to win the prize.

He had a nice face. Really bright eyes. The stubble that showed under his cap was blond, like a golden retriever. I smiled to myself. He was a dog. A good dog — not the nasty ones the guards patrolled with. The sort of dog who'd bring you a stick or an old sock from under the bed, wanting to play.

I didn't have time to play.

"What's he doing here?" I asked Rose when she passed by to see how I was getting on.

"Repairs," she replied. "Don't tell me you've gone gooey too?"

"Ha, ha. I need to get a move on. Francine's almost finished fitting sleeves to her baby-vomit dress."

I was lost in yellow satin when I felt a warm presence looming at my side.

* * *

"Something broken?" said Dog, setting down his toolbox.

"My machine's fine," I said, inching away from his warmth.

"Is that so? Let me have a look . . ."

"Don't get oil on my satin!"

I eased the material free as he poked about with the machine.

Dog tutted. "You're lucky it's still going."

"Really?"

"Terrible tension. Springs too tight. Spools rusted. It should be oiled weekly. Or daily if used a lot — which, I'm guessing, applies to all the machines here."

I flushed with panic. The machine couldn't go wrong now!

"Can you fix it?"

"You better believe I can." He leaned in closer, under pretense of rooting with the tension spring. His voice was a murmur in my ear. "I can fix it so it'll never work again, and the pigs can go sing for their stupid fashions, or go naked for all we care, right?"

"S-sabotage?"

He touched his fingers to his cap in a miniature salute and whispered, "Right first time, ma'am. Won't take a minute."

I glanced back to where the guard was propped against the wall, reading a magazine.

Dog murmured, "I'm Henrik, by the way. What's your name?"

My name? Since when did anyone *here* ask your name instead of a number?

113

"Never mind that. Stop fixing my machine! I mean, stop *breaking* it. I want it to work."

Henrik raised an eyebrow at my tone.

I raised both mine back at him. "I'm a dressmaker. I have to get this gown finished. It's going to be the most beautiful thing I've ever sewn."

Henrik made a mock bow. "Pardon me for thinking you were a slave worker like the rest of us, making fine gowns for mass murderers!"

"I'm not a slave!"

"Oh, do They pay you? Have you got the right to leave whenever you want?"

"No."

"So . . . you're a slave."

I shook my head. "It's Them that call us slaves. I'm *me*. I'm Ella. And I sew."

The mockery slid off Henrik's face. "Good for you!" he said quietly. "I mean it! That's real fighting talk. They can put us in a prison, but they can't capture our spirit, right?"

Marta looked our way, sniffing the air for any hint of a problem. Henrik busied himself with the internal mechanism of my machine, pretending to fix a fault that didn't exist. Before he left, he squeezed my hand.

"Keep strong, Ella. Word from outside is that the War could be over soon. We're fighting back. The good guys are getting closer every day."

Now my heart *did* flip. "We're winning? How do you

know all this? Can you get messages out of Birchwood as well as in? I want to tell my grandma I'm OK." Questions poured out of me.

"Better than that, why not tell her yourself?"

"We're being liberated?"

Henrik leaned closer. "Not exactly. But let's just say there might be a way to liberate yourself."

"*Escape?*"

Henrik clanged his toolbox and put a finger to his lips. "I'll see you again, Ella!"

I watched him as he dodged between the tables to leave. Lucky him, free to wander around as an odd-jobber, just like a normal person. He must have powerful prominents protecting him to have such a role.

"Oh, not you as well?" said Shona, giving me a dig in the ribs as she passed.

I jumped. "Me?"

"Got a thing for the repair guy?" She pinched my cheek and hurried on before Marta started shouting.

It was only when I tried to get back to work on the dress that I realized Henrik had done exactly what I'd asked him not to. My sewing machine was broken.

Marta said I was to deliver Francine's dress to Madam H.

"But *mine's* finished and ready to go," I objected. And it was, thanks to a frenzied burst of hand-sewing on my part. Screw Henrik and his sabotage! How lovingly I had rolled the hem of the gown. How neatly I'd overstitched

115

the seams and finished the neckline. I had forgotten who the dress was for while I was wrapped up in the sewing.

"Just shut up and take it," Marta replied with a nasty twist of her mouth: her version of a smile. She snatched the sunflower dress from me and, soon after, handed me a big flat box.

All the other seamstresses were jealous that I was getting to leave Birchwood. Well, the part of the prison camp we all knew, at any rate. My heart fluttered a little, remembering Henrik's talk of escape. It was impossible, of course. Not dressed as a Stripey, and not with a guard as escort. None other than Carla.

"Nice day for a walk," she said with a wink. Then, "Heel, Pippa, *heel.*" The dog had spotted a herd of Stripeys and was itching to go scatter them.

I trotted to heel like the hound. I wasn't on a leash, but I might as well have been. We were in full sight of Birchwood's sentry towers and machine guns. Sun shone on twists of barbed wire. Guards were everywhere, and bosses too. There was no escaping the sight of miserable work gangs, lugging lumps of stone by hand or digging ditches in full sun. Every single worker was just a skeleton in a striped sack. They'd all been women once.

My arms ached miserably. I had to hold the cardboard dress box flat. I was terrified of dropping it, much as I fantasized about spilling Francine's frumpy dress onto the road so *my* frock would go to Madam H. instead.

It was good to be outside, though, more or less. The air was somehow fresher when it wasn't trapped behind barbed wire, even if it was still tainted with the taste of petrol, ash, and smoke. There were clear views over fields cropped down to dead yellow stubble. I could see a distant streak of brown, coming closer by the second. Another train arriving.

I remembered Henrik's talk of escape. Imagine that — just kicking off these stupid wooden shoes and running out to the fields . . . *free!*

Carla's bullets would reach me before the dog did, *bang, bang, bang* in my back.

The strangest sight for me was all the *men*. They looked just as tired and ragged as the women workers.

"Good to get away from the crowds," said Carla to me or Pippa; I couldn't be sure which. "Summer's been rotten! All those *hordes* arriving at the station, so no hope of a seaside holiday to get away from this *heat. Ten thousand* units a day to process, can you believe it? What do they think we are? Machines?"

I blinked rapidly. *Units?* Drops of sweat were rolling into my eyes, and I had no free hand to wipe them away.

"And Pippa needs her walkies, doesn't she, darling? Doesn't she, drippy chops? Who's the best doggie, then? Hey? Hey? Who's the best?"

I had to stop walking while Carla fussed over the mutt. When I looked down there was a tiny mole at my feet. It was dead. The first creature I'd seen in months that wasn't a dog, a rat, a louse, or a bedbug. It reminded me of Grandma's moleskin slippers, all soft and patchy where the fur had worn away.

Pippa came to sniff at the mole corpse. Carla yanked the leash.

We came to a wrought-iron gate. It was scrolled in beautiful loops, like something from a storybook. A Stripey ran up to let us in. Carla ignored him. She clearly knew her way. Pippa stopped to piddle by a gatepost.

I followed Carla down a garden path. I tripped on almost every paving stone, I was so busy gazing at the wonderland. There were flowers everywhere. Not just ones printed on fabric, or embroidered with silks. Real flowers! They grew in abundant borders around the edge of a lawn grown from real grass. Every blade of grass within Birchwood's barbed wire had been eaten.

At the edge of the lawn, two tortoises were munching at a feast of vegetable peelings. I stared at them, mesmerized. Watering the lawn was a Stripey gardener with a hose. I got sprinkled with water drops. It reminded me of a summer's afternoon years and years ago when Grandad leaned out of an upstairs window while I was in the yard below, and he showered me and my friends from a watering can. We'd squealed so much! No squealing now. I had to step out of the way of a little boy clattering past on a bicycle — the same boy I'd once seen in the fitting room with Madam H. He left scuff marks on the lawn.

"Hurry up," grouched Carla.

I trotted after her, pausing just long enough to smell the yellow roses growing right next to the door.

Pippa was told to *sit, stay* outside.

Then a real hallway in a real house. I smelled beeswax furniture polish, fried fish, and the lingering ghost of freshly baked bread. Farther up and farther in: carpets on the floor, woven with happy colors.

A door opened somewhere deeper in the house. There was a patter of feet. Not a dog running—a toddler. A real child scampering around noisily. A voice called out. The toddler must have tiptoed after that, because everything went silent.

Another door opened. A girl stood there, framed by the white gloss paintwork. She was just a couple of years younger than I was, with a fresh dress made of yellow checked cotton. She had a bow in her brown hair and a book in her hand. I saw her eyes go straight to the dress box.

"Mother's in the sitting room," she said to Carla, never noticing me at all. Then she walked off in light summer sandals.

Yet another door along the hall. Carla knocked.

"Come in!" said a woman within. When the door opened, I saw a sitting room decorated in soft vanillas and pastel shades of lemon. There was a bookcase . . .

"A *bookcase?*" Rose couldn't keep quiet any longer. "What books were there?"

"Who's telling this story?" I objected.

Rose pretended to pout. "Strictly speaking it's a descriptive narrative, not a story, because it's true. It is true, isn't it? About the books? Oh, we used to have a room just full of books in our palace. All four walls, with a space for the door. There was a ladder on wheels that you could roll along to reach every shelf. *That* was traveling, Ella — from history to botany to tales of wonder and imagination . . ."

"You and your make-believe palace. Hush now, or don't you want to hear the rest?"

"Yeah, shut your mouth for once," laughed Girder. She was hunched on the edge of the bunk below, scarfing black-market bread and swigging black-market booze. "We want to hear about the commandant's house."

"And the boy!" someone shouted with a hoarse voice. "Tell us about the little boy — how old? My son was three when They took us."

This audience for stories had begun weeks before, with Rose spinning her tales from the top bunk. Nearby Stripeys had swayed toward the sound of her voice, like sunflowers turning to the light. Rose's reputation had spread. Stripeys came crawling across the bunks to hear her better. Girder soon demanded a story.

"I don't think I can do the sort of stories you like," Rose had said cautiously. Girder knew the rudest, lewdest songs of anyone in Birchwood.

Girder said, "Just tell 'em like you have been. With the

woodcutters, the wolves, and swords that cut stone — I fancy getting me one of those, ha!"

Now that I had ventured beyond the gates of Birchwood and lived to tell the tale, I had been ordered — by Rose *and* Girder — to give a full report.

"The commandant has five children, including a baby," I told everyone. "There was a cradle in the sitting room, covered in lace and ribbons and a cot blanket."

"Oh, my baby boy's cot blanket!" came the lament of the upset mother. "I used to snuggle into that and smell his warm skin and talcum powder . . ."

I swallowed. "I saw toys for older children on the sofa. Toy cars and a doll . . ."

"Did you get to *sit?*" asked Girder. "Big though my buttocks are, I really miss cushions!"

Of course I wasn't allowed to sit. I wasn't even allowed *into* that elegant room. Carla left me alone in the hall with the heavy dress box. I stared at the sprigs of meadow flowers on the wallpaper and the framed photograph of the commandant. If I hadn't known who he was, I'd've said he seemed reliable and handsome, in his civilian suit, lit by the film-star flash of a photographer's studio. It made me wonder what my father had looked like. The man I'd never met. When I got home, perhaps I could find him, and my mother. I'd have a proper family again. Family was important.

The commandant looked like a family man.

"How are you, my dear?" came the voice of the woman in the sitting room. So Madam H. knew Carla already. "Feeling any better after our little chat the other day?" Madam murmured. "I know it's hard missing the farm and your family. Keep doing your duty, and you'll have your reward."

Did the female guards talk with Madam like she was their mother? Soon they spoke too softly for me to hear. Eventually Carla said more loudly, "The dress is here. You know, made by the prisoner I recommended."

I stiffened. So all this time Carla had been pretending to be my friend, when she was actually promoting Francine's work!

At this point in my description of the visit, Girder described Carla in a word that Grandma would never tolerate me *thinking*, let alone saying out loud. It was a very descriptive, emphatic word.

"Oh, there's more," I told my barrack-block audience. "Just wait . . ."

Madam H. came out into the hall. She was wearing a nice summer dress in corn-yellow muslin. Despite feeling horribly tired, I was forced to trot after her and Carla, up two flights of stairs and along a corridor to a back attic room. The room had a bare floor, a table, a chair, a double wardrobe with mirrored doors, and a sewing basket. The window was shut.

The doors to the wardrobe were open. Inside was a feast of fashion. Gowns of every color hung from satin-padded hangers. Short, long, narrow, full — every style was there. Some I recognized from projects at the Upper Tailoring Studio. Some could have come straight from couture houses in the City of Light. Other outfits were hung on the side of the wardrobe. Summer dresses, summer suits, nighties and naughties . . .

Close up, Madam was not the sophisticated aristocratic type I'd imagined. She bustled about looking more distracted than divine. When she took off her day frock she was wearing very sensible underwear and a rubber girdle. A little roll of flesh oozed over the top of it.

I set the dress box on the table and eased the lid off.

Madam gestured me out of the way. She teased apart the leaves of tissue paper packing the dress. Carla stood at the door with her arms folded. I waited to see the disappointment on Madam's face when Francine's excuse of a frock was revealed. Instead her eyes lit up and she practically glowed with pleasure.

"Oh, this is just *ravishing*," she said breathlessly.

Carla smirked. The dress in the box was my very own sunflower gown.

"Marta *tricked* you?" asked my audience in the barrack block.

"What are the odds?" said Girder drily.

* * *

123

Madam held the yellow sunflower dress in front of her and swished from side to side, mesmerized by her own charms.

"Quick, quick," she commanded abruptly. "Help me on with it."

It fit oh-so-beautifully. Perhaps it needed a few minor tweaks here and there. Marta had at least trusted me with pins, so I made the necessary adjustments—or tried to, while Madam turned and turned in front of the mirror. She opened her mouth, then closed it, then opened it again, like a goldfish. One of those fat fish that go around in circles in a pond.

I wondered if goldfish were edible.

Madam gazed for a long time at the ripe beauty of the sunflower embroidery. I was bursting with pride on Rose's behalf.

Finally Madam said, "This is *outstanding*. A perfect fit . . . superlative fabric draping. Tell the woman who made it I am pleased. I will be wanting more from her."

I coughed. Carla nodded at me—*Tell her.*

I almost couldn't rustle up a voice. "Pardon me, Madam. *I* made it."

Now Madam turned and actually looked at me for the first time.

"You? You're just a girl!"

"I'm sixteen," I lied quickly.

Madam turned back to the mirror. "Honestly, I never knew Your Sort were so gifted. Such a piece of luck I set up the Tailoring Studio so your talents wouldn't go to waste, don't you think? After the War, you must all work in a proper couture house, and I shall order my gowns there. How about that?"

She spoke as if there were no Lists, no chimneys, and no ash showers.

"So," said Rose, back in the barrack block, "how does it feel to be the most amazing dress designer ever?"

To her surprise—to everyone's surprise, even my own—I burst into tears.

"You're a lucky girl," said Marta, somehow making it sound like a threat. "I decided your dress was acceptable for Madam after all. You've learned a lot working for me. Of course, I did train in all the very best places."

I was trying not to flaunt my success in front of all the other seamstresses. Trying and failing.

Marta folded her arms so her sharp elbows stuck out. Was it my imagination, or did she actually look *amused* at my happiness?

"Madam says you can make more things for her."

"I will," I said quickly. "She won't be disappointed. I already have lots of ideas."

"Ideas don't buy bread. Get sewing. I've got you a replacement machine from the Department Store, since you broke the last one."

"Thank you. I'll start right away."

"Eager beaver!" Marta said, with that twist of her mouth that resembled a smile.

I sat down in a daze. Rose would be glad she'd embroidered the sunflower. We'd get maybe as many as six cigarettes as a reward — we'd be like millionaires! We could plan the next few outfits together, my designs, her —

I looked at the new sewing machine and froze.

"Need a hand setting it up?" mumbled Shona across the aisle, pin in her mouth. "Ella? I said, do you need any help with the new machine?" She took the pin out, jammed it in a length of custard-colored cotton, then succumbed to a coughing fit.

I shook my head. There were words, but they wouldn't come out as human speech. *No, thank you. I know exactly how to thread this machine. I ought to. I've done it a million times before. It's my grandmother's, after all.*

There it sat, lid off, gleaming in black-enamel glory with swirls of gold decoration. A line of writing had been scratched off, exactly where Grandma's name had been engraved.

Grandma never let a speck of fluff or dust settle on her machine. I lifted the sewing foot and saw that it was beautifully clean beneath.

She was always orderly with her threads, too. I opened the lid to the bobbin compartment to reveal neat rows of tiny steel reels — green, yellow, red, gray, white, and pink.

Cautiously I peered around the side. Just as I remembered: faint scratch marks on the enamel where Grandma's wedding ring used to catch when she made adjustments.

I sat there. Paralyzed.

It couldn't be *here*, in Birchwood. Not Betty, the sewing machine Grandma loved so much she'd given it a name. Betty was in her sewing room at home. It was on the table where it had always been, next to her chair with the chewed-up foam cushion, by the window with the daisy-patterned curtains.

Rose found an excuse to come by.

"Are you all right?" she whispered. "You look sick."

I couldn't even look at her. I was picturing Grandma trudging down the street to the station in her block-heeled shoes, tilting to the left to balance the weight of the machine case in her right hand. *Bring food for the journey, warm clothes and essential items,* she'd've been told. Of course she'd consider Betty essential.

I knew only too well what They did to new arrivals at Birchwood. How you had to take all your clothes off. *Fold them neatly!* the guards shouted, as if you'd be out of the shower room all clean and ready to wear them again. How you had to stand with hundreds of strangers, naked and shaking with embarrassment. Didn't matter if you were fat or thin, young or old, pregnant, on your period, or plain petrified. You waited there naked while Stripeys came at you with dull razors to shave your hair. Then you went through the next doors—always *hurry, hurry, hurry*—and then . . .

For me, and others considered fit to work, a cold shower. A single garment flung at each of us, and a headscarf. A pair of stupid wooden shoes which, by chance or malice, were always the wrong size, or random shoes thrown from the pile left by the last lot of people to be processed. Then *out, out, out* to the quarantine block, where we huddled and cried and waited for the chance to get a job. To survive.

For me, work. Life.

"I'm fine," I lied to Rose. She gave my hand a quick squeeze and darted back to her ironing.

I sat looking at the machine. It was Betty.

Marta's voice cut through my thoughts, sharp as lemon juice on a scrape. "Is there a problem, Ella?"

"No, no problem. Just getting back to work now. Right now."

I pushed material under the new machine's sewing foot and let the stitches run on and on and on, if only to hear the sound of my childhood once more. As it whirred away, I was back in Grandma's room, a little girl again, picking up pins from the carpet.

Use the back of your hand to find pins on the floor, Grandma said. *That way it doesn't hurt when you find them and they prick.*

Would I bleed to death from a pinprick? I'd asked her.

Don't be a daftie, she'd said.

I had a child-high view of Grandma's round legs, the worn moleskin slippers, the hem of her cotton print dress. All just memories, as insubstantial as dreams.

When work was over and we lined for soup-water, Rose scratched away at my sadness, like a squirrel digging for a buried nut. Finally I told her what was wrong, quietly so no one else could hear. She listened without interrupting.

"What's worst is, I can't even tell if it *is* Betty or not," I said at the end of my tale, trying hard to keep my voice down. "I ought to know! Rose, I'm starting to forget what Grandma and Grandad look like!"

A guard passed by. We fell silent. The guard went out of sight.

Rose whispered, "You don't really forget. All the memories go somewhere safe, I promise. I've been imagining walking around every room in the palace and every tree in the orchard back home. I pretend I'm reading the book titles in the palace library, but there are so many I can't remember. Then I listen for the sound of my papa coming home. He was in the army — an officer of course. He always smelled of horses, and had dogs surging around his riding boots. Proper dogs, that wag tails and want to be friends, not the monsters They have here. But I can't remember if his eyes are medium-brown or light brown. At least I *think* they were brown . . ."

We were at the front of the line. Soup-water was slopped into our tin bowls. I looked at the gritty gray water and the single coil of potato peeling. It was easier than looking around at the Stripeys, searching and hoping not to spot Grandma's face under every headscarf.

"Are you going to eat that soup or memorize it?" Rose teased.

I circled my spoon around and around the lukewarm liquid.

"What if she was arrested—Grandma, and Grandad too?"

"You just have to hope they're safe and well, Ella."

"What if we're here alive and having soup, but they're . . . ?"

"Shh. Don't say it. Have hope."

I tried it out, to see how it felt. Hope would mean that Rose was right. That the sewing machine wasn't Betty at all, and that Grandma and Grandad were still fine.

Hope.

Red

The sun set with streaks of scarlet. Even summer nights must grow dark. Invisible in the straw of our bunk, I was glad no one could see me crying like a little baby. Rose put her skinny arms around me and kissed my shaved head. I wiped my eyes and nose on my sleeve like some dirty beggar girl.

"I was dreaming," I told Rose, in between sniffs and snuffles.

"Were you back at home?"

I had that dream sometimes—waking up in my bed at home and hearing Grandad clattering about in the kitchen, washing dishes. It was worse than the nightmares, because I had to wake up and remember it wasn't true.

"No. I was back at Madam's house, in that attic sewing room. The dress was there, soaking up a pool of blood. Really deep, sticky red blood. I looked in the mirror and saw myself—just a load of bones fastened together with skin, in this horrible striped dress and these awful *ugly* shoes! You know, we weren't disgusting until we came here. They *made* us this way, then they sneer at us. They make us live like rats in a sewer and wonder why we stink!"

"I know, I know," Rose crooned, still holding me close. "It's not fair, dear."

"Not fair?" I would've sat up in fury if that hadn't meant banging my head on the rafters above. "Not *fair?* It's completely *evil*, that's what it is. I *hate* being one of the ugly ones! Why can't *we* have the nice things and live in posh houses? Madam sleeps on a comfy mattress with lace-edged pillows, Carla gets to gorge on cookies and read fashion magazines, and we're . . . we're *here* . . ."

In the dark I heard the rustle of straw and the cries of someone else suffering. I felt something crawl over my neck. A louse. These little beasts loved the cracks in our skin and the seams of our clothes. They drank our blood until they were fat and swollen. I slapped it into a splodge of red.

"I'm sorry, Rose, so sorry. I made you sew that sunflower and you knew it was wrong. You've known all along we're making magic for the wrong people. They shouldn't have our beautiful talents. They don't deserve them."

"Beauty is still beauty," she said.

"Not on a . . . a . . . turd, it isn't. *What?* Why are you laughing?"

"Sorry, I can't help it!" she choked. "The image of Madam as a big poop in a silk gown, twirling around on the commandant's arm . . . It's just too disgusting and too hilarious."

"Glad you think *something's* funny," I said woefully.

That set Rose off giggling even more. It was contagious.

I began to laugh too. Have you ever been desperate to stop laughing, because it's driving everyone else mad, and making your ribs hurt, and because you really don't feel that happy anyway? That's how it was. In the end we just clutched each other until the silly-shakes stopped.

When we were finally still Rose gave a big, deep sigh. "Poor you," she whispered. "Here, don't tell anyone: I've got a present for you."

Her hand found mine in the dark. I felt something soft.

"What is it?" I whispered back.

"A ribbon. You'll see in the morning. A piece of beauty, just for you."

"Rosalind, this is *silk*. How on earth did you pay for it? You *never* manage to get cigarettes for barter."

Her voice had a smirk in it. "You'll be proud of me, Ella. I stole it from the Department Store."

"*Stole it?*"

"Shh—don't tell everyone!"

"I seem to remember some smug missus telling me, *Ooh, don't you know stealing's wrong?*"

"Never mind about that now," said Rose. "Keep it safe, and remember that one day we'll be out of here and wearing as many ribbons as we like. We'll go to the City of Light and tie this little ribbon to the branch of a tree I know—it can mean hope for us."

Hope. Now there's a word.

* * *

You couldn't ever say you'd had a good night's sleep in Birchwood. Only the dead were peaceful. I did at least have a few dreamless hours. When I woke, I felt for the ribbon.

In the center of the barrack block, the light bulb flickered into life, and Girder's whistle blew.

"*Out, out, out, you lazy mares!*" she shouted. "Rise and shine, for another day in paradise!"

In the harsh light I saw that the ribbon was red. I put it in the little secret pocket-bag I'd made to go under my dress and climbed down from the bunk. I paused. Took the ribbon out. Looked at it. Put it back.

We ran to the toilet block to fight for facilities. How often had I rolled out of bed at home for a wash in warm water, to get dressed in clean clothes and to share breakfast before school with Grandma and Grandad? Now I was just another panicked animal, without even the luxury of a facecloth.

We stumbled out into the morning and lined up in fives for roll call. Thousands and thousands of us, all striped, ragged, anonymous. I couldn't stand it. I *knew* it was stupid, but I carefully pulled the red ribbon out of my pocket-bag and knotted it in a bow around my neck.

Because I was just stupid, not completely insane, I tugged at the top of my dress to hide the ribbon.

I looked across at Rose and winked. She winked back. She hadn't seen what I'd done. Beyond the building roofs and barbed-wire fences, the most beautiful sunrise was touching everything with a soft red glow. It lit a skyful of clouds that promised a cooler day. There was even the hope of refreshing rain.

I almost didn't mind that roll call was dragging on and on and on. As usual the bosses did most of the counting. The guards stood around complaining about the early rising, and about how horribly bored they were. Then one guard broke away from the black huddle and began a random check along the ranks of five. Like everyone else I kept my chin up and my eyes down. The dogs were out — hungry and restless.

I smelled something sweet above the usual Birchwood stink. The sort of scent a lady might wear to a smoky city nightclub at midnight, not what a guard at Birchwood should be wearing for roll call at five in the morning.

Carla stopped in front of me. My nose twitched. I kept my gaze on her jacket buttons.

Then I remembered the ribbon. My heart contracted. I'd tied it low enough, hadn't I? She wouldn't see it. Anyway, it was only Carla.

The leather on Carla's gloved hand creaked as she reached forward and dragged my neckline down.

"What's that?" she asked sweetly. "Answer me! What is it?"

"A ribbon."

"A ribbon. Yes, I can see that. What I really want to know is, why are *you* wearing it?"

Now was the time to apologize. To grovel. To yank the ribbon off and hang my head in defeat.

But the ribbon gave me a terrible confidence.

"I wanted to look pretty."

"What was that?" Carla leaned in so close I thought I'd choke on her perfume. "I didn't quite catch what you said."

Had the whole world suddenly gone silent?

I lifted my chin. "I said, I wanted to look pretty."

Whack!

I was so surprised I didn't even realize what had happened. It was a bit like the time I'd been sitting at the front of a bus when it ran into a pigeon. This time Carla's hand had apparently run into my head. No feathers or blood, at least.

My ears were ringing, and I stumbled to the side. Pippa yelped — one paw trodden on.

"Pretty?" Carla mocked. "Like a *monkey* in mascara? Like a *rat* in lipstick?"

Whack! The second blow. My brain seemed to slosh from side to side. I touched my broken lip and saw red on my fingertips. Every instinct said *FIGHT BACK*. All I could do was stand at attention.

Whack! A third blow, and Pippa was growling now.

Drops of rain started to spatter down.

"Please! Don't! It was me! *I* gave it to her. It's my ribbon, my fault!"

Shut up, Rose, keep your head down, and keep out of this.

Whack! Carla turned and hit Rose so hard she toppled into the next woman along, and she fell on the next, and I thought the whole row of Stripeys would go over like dominoes.

138

Rose landed in the dust. Dark spots of rain blotched her dress. With Carla there looming, no one dared help her up. I moved to do just that. Rose shook her head.

"How *touching*." Carla practically spat the words out. "Willing to lie for a friend." She pulled a black boot back, ready to kick. That was too much for me.

"Leave her alone! She hasn't done anything! *I'm* the one with the ribbon!"

Carla looked me straight in the face and kicked Rose in the stomach. Next she took up her looped whip. Because of the prisoners all around, there wasn't room to crack the whip fully, so Carla started beating me with the handle, then with her fists, then, once I was down on the ground, with her boots. Each time Rose tried to intervene, she got kicked too.

I tucked my knees to my chest and covered my head with my arms, trying to make myself as small as possible. *It's me*, I wanted to shriek. *Me! Ella! The girl you've been chatting to for weeks. The girl you fed cake to. The girl who makes your gorgeous clothes.*

Rain fell more heavily, mingling with blood. Dust turned to mud.

There was a pause. The sound of heavy breathing.

When I dared look, I saw that Carla's face was twisted up like paper kindling on a fire, waiting to burn. Her eyes seemed to have shrunk to little glass beads. Water ran down her cheeks in a parody of tears.

139

"You dirty pig-dog beast!" she shouted. Spittle flew out of her mouth. "You vermin, scum, filth on my feet!"

Sick with pain, I tried to shift over to where Rose lay, in that forest of bony legs and stripy skirts. She reached out a hand to me. I stretched mine out too.

Carla shrieked, "Did you really think you could be pretty like *me*? I don't need you and your stupid sewing to make me beautiful. You're nothing! Nobody! Subhuman! I don't care about you at all! You might as well be *dead*!"

With that final explosion of rage she lifted her boot and brought it smashing down on my outstretched hand.

"Ella? Ella? Get up, Ella!"

Grandma was shaking me. I was late for school! Late for a test! The most important exam ever and I didn't know the questions and hadn't studied at all and I couldn't even find the exam room with my eyes swollen shut like this . . .

"Ella!"

Somebody was hauling me upright — not Grandma and Grandad, two strangers, I thought. I squinted. Saw stripes. Smelled blood.

That voice again: "Ella, stay standing up! Ella — are you OK?"

I would be if the world would stop whirling round.

"I'm fine," I said, in a blood-filled voice. "You?"

"Fine," whispered Rose. Then, I suppose because us being *fine* was so ludicrously untrue, a quiet laugh burst out of her, quickly smothered. I half laughed too. It made blood bubble in my nose.

When roll call was finally over, we staggered through summer rain with the rest of the Stripey herd. Rose had to lead me; I was still half-blind and doubled over.

At the workshop we headed straight for the sink. The guard stepped up to see what the commotion was, then backed away in disgust when she noticed my injuries. Thank goodness Marta wasn't around yet.

"Don't drip on the sewing," Rose said, only half joking. There was a trail of red spots on the floor behind me.

The others crowded close—*What happened? Who did this? Are you OK?*

I spat blood into the running water at the sink. "I'm fine. Rose is fine. You are fine, aren't you, Rose?"

"Don't worry about me. Let's clean you up."

Brigid the hedgehog passed over a damp cloth. Rose dabbed at my face. I started shaking. It was only when I tried to push her away that I became aware of the heavy throb of pain in my hand. The hand Carla had stomped on.

"Look at it," said Francine in awe. "It's wrecked."

"Don't be stupid," snapped Rose. "It'll be bruised. Sprained. Nothing serious."

I tucked my hand close to my chest and whimpered, like a wounded animal.

"Sorry, Ella, we've got to wash it and bind it up."

Rose did that quickly. She was so brave that I didn't dare cry either. We hadn't any bandages so I unknotted the red ribbon with my good hand and passed it to her. Not once did she tell me off for daring to wear it. Not once did she say the beatings were my fault, even though I knew they were. She used the ribbon to bind my fingers straight between two pieces of stolen card. I swayed at the pain.

Next we hid the ribbon bandage under a square of old cotton. Hardly the best first aid ever, but the best I'd get in Birchwood. Despite the awful throbbing in my fingers, I liked the feel of that red ribbon: hope was still there, just out of sight.

"Marta could be back at any moment. We can't let her see Ella's so injured," said Shona. "You remember Rhoda?"

Everyone nodded. They remembered.

"That was the woman who worked here before me?" I asked.

"She was an amazing cutter. It was like material just melted between the shears. There was nobody like her."

"So what happened?"

"Just a stupid mistake. She cut her finger. It went septic. She got sick with blood poisoning. Marta could maybe have gotten her medicine, but she said it wasn't worth it. Rhoda went to the Hospital."

There was a murmur of fear and disgust around the room. The Hospital was a last resort.

"Marta wouldn't let her come back?" I asked.

Francine shrugged. "Rhoda's place got filled."

"By me."

"By you. The Hospital got full. They cleared it to make room for new patients. That was the end of Rhoda." Francine sprinkled her fingers to show ash falling. "So, like Shona said, keep that hand hidden from Marta if you can."

Right on cue, Marta the shark slid out from the fitting room and glided between the workbenches, scattering smaller fish.

"What's all this? Why aren't you working, Ella? You think because Madam likes one dress you can take a holiday? Ugh! How can I send you into the fitting room with a face like that? What have you got there?"

"Nothing."

"You're hiding something."

"Just my hand."

"What's wrong with your hand?"

"Nothing's wrong."

"Show me. *Now*. Good god, you idiot—why did you let that happen?"

"Nothing's broken. It's just bruised."

"Bruised or broken, you're hardly any use to me now," Marta cried. "Oh, come on, you aren't seriously thinking you can *sew* with one hand?"

My face flamed even redder than before. "No, not for a couple of days, maybe."

"A couple of days? You'll be lucky to lift a needle ever again—"

"She just needs to let it heal, that's all," Rose interrupted. "She can still supervise, and sketch designs with her other hand."

Marta didn't even pretend to think it over. "This is a sewing salon, not a rest home or artists' retreat. She goes. In fact, you both go."

I couldn't believe what I was hearing.

"Rose did the sunflower on Madam's dress. She's the best embroiderer here."

Marta shrugged. "There are hundreds of women in Birchwood who can sew flowers. Just the same as there are hundreds of cutters and dressmakers. New prisoners arriving every day, too. I can have my pick of those."

"Aw, c'mon, Marta," said Francine. "Clients like Ella's work. Madam was crazy about her sunflower dress, remember?"

I vowed there and then to worship Francine forever after. And maybe pass her some cigarettes and extra bread too. And paper for the toilet.

"Ella's the best," said Shona, in between raspy coughs. Brigid nodded, wordless as ever.

"Besides," said Francine, "aren't we all family here in the sewing room? We should stick together."

Marta was having none of it. "Our families are *dead*, and I didn't get to be a prominent by being soft. Now *get out*, you two . . . or do I have to ask the guard to whip you out?"

She was serious. She was actually going to toss us both!

144

I tried shaking my head at the injustice, but it hurt too much. "After all I've done for you?" I spluttered.

Not one scrap of emotion colored her face. Not one spark of pity lit her eyes. Like Rabbit-woman all those months before, Rose and I were to be thrown to the wolves. Away from the sanctuary of the workshop, we'd be at the mercy of the guards, the weather, and the relentless back-breaking labor squads. It was bad enough sewing on the pitiful rations we had. Doing hard labor would kill us slowly — if guards didn't kill us quickly.

What would Marta do?

No need to speculate: she'd just done it.

We were out.

We stood, bruised and aching, on the doorstep to the workroom. I winced as the door slammed behind us. The air outside was wet and gritty. A work gang of Stripeys went hurrying past with planks of wood hoisted on their shoulders. Next came Stripeys with wheelbarrows of cement, on the double. All kept their heads down and their eyes on the ground. Guards screamed at them to go *faster, faster.*

"What shall we do?" Rose whispered. "If we don't work we'll be . . . *you know.*" She flicked a quick look up to the stark chimneys towering high over the camp.

I tried to straighten up. Just that simple movement made me crazy with pain.

"Maybe we should get you to the Hospital!" cried Rose.

"No! Didn't you hear Shona? They don't cure people there; it's just a waiting room for . . . for the end."

I definitely did *not* look at the chimneys. I tried not to think about the fact that if Rhoda hadn't gone to the Hospital, there'd never have been a job for me at the workshop.

I took a breath, tasting iron as blood trickled down my throat. My hand hurt so much it felt like it was on fire. I could feel the ribbon, though.

"You know what, Rose? My grandma always says, 'If the sun isn't shining, make the most of rain.'"

"It certainly is raining," Rose said, wiping drops from her face.

"It's like one of your stories, where the characters in the middle of it are having a terrible time and it seems impossible that they'll ever get through it, but they do."

"If we were in a story, I'd whistle up an eagle to fly us both out of here, straight to the City of Light. We'd be dropped in a fountain for a wash, then whisked away in a luxury motorcar, straight to a cake shop."

I heard dogs barking. "Your eagle's late. I say we run to the barrack block, hide in the bunk till roll call, then bribe Girder to find us a new job as quickly as possible."

"One where there's no chance of meeting Carla again," Rose suggested.

"Unless one of us has a large frying pan handy," I replied grimly.

I was thinking of the time Grandma got up in the night, convinced there were burglars. She had the frying pan in one hand and an old hockey stick in the other. Terrifying. She'd been almost disappointed to find it was just a stray cat that had come in through an open window.

Rose smiled. "You know, Ella, I never told you what sort of animal you remind me of."

"Go on then," I said warily.

"You're a fox."

"A *fox*?"

"Why not? A fox is loyal to a small family, a cunning survivor, and it adapts to any environment. Foxes have sharp teeth to attack and defend, but they're soft and warm for cuddling. Farmers hate them, but you can't have everything."

I suppose that wasn't so bad. I took Rose's hand with my uninjured one, so we stood like an old-fashioned gentleman and lady.

"Shall we, my dear?"

She nodded. "Dearest, we shall."

Hand in hand, we stepped into the mud and set out to survive together.

Gray

Rose and I faced a monstrous instrument of torture. A machine with hand cranks, metal cogs, and wooden rollers. Steam filled the air. Behind us, our new boss-woman grunted. She loomed like a big brown bear on its hind paws, not sure whether to swipe us flat and chew on us, or lumber off and leave us alive. She jerked her head toward the machine.

"Work!"

It was the first word we'd heard her speak. Her eyes were small, dull stones without the slightest shine of intelligence.

Rose rolled up her sleeves, revealing biceps no bigger than bee stings. She set her arms to the big crank at one side of the machine. Bear growled. As best I could with only one decent hand, I took a folded bedsheet and began to feed it between the machine's rollers. Rose set her entire strength against the crank. The rollers barely budged. The handle jerked. Rose lurched, and the machine gobbled at the sheet, dragging me with it. I let go of the sheet before I got pulled through the rollers. They didn't call this machine a mangle for nothing.

Bear roared. The sheet was stuck halfway through the mangle, creased even worse than before.

"We can do it" I said, wiping sweat from my face. "We just need to practice. We haven't worked a mangle before."

"Never seen a mangle before!" shrieked a Stripey who followed Bear around like her shadow. She had a laugh like a hyena. It was already driving me insane. "Don't know how to work it! Not so fine and fancy now, eh? Not so primped and proud—ha, ha, ha!"

Rose turned and raised an eyebrow. Hyena's laugh dwindled.

Bear looked from me to the mangle, then to Rose. She shook her head. "Outside!" she said.

"No, really," I answered quickly. "We're very quick learners. Show us how to do it."

"*Outside!*"

Hyena giggled.

Day one at Birchwood laundry and we were already failures.

"My grandma always said if you want to get out of doing a job, pretend to do it badly," I told Rose under my breath. "That's how come Grandad never asked us to help when the drains were blocked or the roof gutters needed cleaning. Not after we'd *helped* him so badly the first time around."

Rose grinned. "No need to pretend to botch things when it comes to this job!"

* * *

They called it the Washery. It wasn't a laundry for Stripeys, of course, just for the guards and officers. It was a squat gray complex with stone floors and flooding drains, built around a cobbled yard. There were no washing machines. Why waste electricity when you had Stripeys to do all the hard work by hand?

About thirty women worked slapping gray shirts on washboards, swirling green-gray trousers in tubs, and rinsing gray knickers under taps.

"Rub the gussets! Rub the gussets!" Hyena called.

Bear prodded us toward a door. Hyena trotted behind.

I made one more appeal to be given a job indoors. "Look, we know there's a Mending Room here. Both of us are professional sewers. We could do that work beautifully. I made clothes for Madam H. herself."

Bear stopped next to a giant wicker basket. She picked something out of the basket and threw it at me. A wet pair of underpants splatted on my face. Hyena cackled. I peeled the pants off and gripped them tightly. I was *this* close to lobbing them back at Bear.

Rose said hurriedly, "You'd like us to hang the laundry out? Wonderful. It's a nice fresh day for it, don't you think? We'll just need clothespins . . . and if you could be so kind as to show us where the washing lines are . . . marvelous."

Rose's posh accent and politeness totally flummoxed

153

our new boss. Bear kicked the wicker basket and grunted at Hyena, who said, "I'll show you the drying ground. And here's clothespins. Lots of clothespins. Clip them on, look!" Hyena put two on her ear lobes, one on her nose, and laughed again.

I didn't know whether to laugh or cry. Was it so crazy to be crazy in a place like Birchwood?

The biggest laundry baskets were on wheels. We had to push them to the drying ground, pin everything out, then stand—bored out of our minds—while the washing dried. I couldn't use the fingers on my damaged hand, so Rose had to help, and she was barely tall enough to reach the line. More than one piece of washing went down into the dust. We shook things clean as best we could and carried on.

Our arms ached and our bruises still throbbed. That didn't matter. Thanks to an outrageously high bribe paid to Girder, we'd been set up at the Washery just one day after being booted out by Marta. It was pretty cushy by Birchwood standards—though far below being in the Department Store, the kitchens, or the Upper Tailoring Studio.

We were alive and the sun was shining.

In between the flapping sheets, we could look past Birchwood's barbed wire to where farmers gathered in the harvest as free people. Summer was almost over. I gazed out over the shorn fields to a line of smoke puffs. "I see a train. There aren't so many arriving now, are there?"

Rose was gazing up at puffs of cloud. "I can see a dragon, a fairy, a goblet, and, if you squint a bit, that cloud looks just like a crown."

"Or a meat pie."

"Oh, *pie* . . ." said Rose with a sigh.

From the drying ground we could even see the faraway roofs of houses and shops.

Instead of brooding about Betty the sewing machine having been transplanted into the Upper Tailoring Studio, I liked to imagine Grandma and Grandad sitting down at the kitchen table to eat. The kitchen stools had cushions that blew out rude noises when sat on. Every single time this happened, Grandad never failed to make a face that said, *It wasn't me!*

At teatime there'd be thick slices of bread and honey, boiled eggs sprinkled with salt, and tiny, briny lamb sausages. After that, cake. I could never decide what sort of cake I'd eat first when the War was over and I got home. I definitely hoped there'd be a cake shop next to my dress shop in the City of Light. Rose said there would be. She confidently predicted endless iced buns. Even though I knew she was just making it all up, she sounded very convincing. I just wished imaginary cakes were as filling as real ones.

The view from the drying ground—and the thought of food—made me ache for freedom. Not so much Rose. She told me she was always free, in that strange story land inside her head. She passed the hours telling me tall tales of her life in a palace as a countess, with her mother scribbling books or dancing with dukes and her father fighting duels at dawn and tanks by teatime. It was all quite convincing, even though I knew it had to be made up.

But the most astonishing story I heard in that summer's dying days was one about Marta. And, unbelievably, it was true.

The women at the Washery weren't into Rose's stories. They liked *gossip*, the more shocking and scandalous the better. We got used to hearing who was in love with whom. Who were best friends, who were worst enemies. Which guards were up for promotion; which guards were pregnant. I thought it was all horrible. Then one day Marta's name came up.

"You mean Marta from the Upper Tailoring Studio?" I asked. "Nose so sharp you could file your nails on it?"

The main gossip, a shriveled-up girl I called Shrew, glared at me for butting in. I glared back. I had perfected a pretty good mean stare since working at the Washery (inspired by Marta herself).

"Might be her," said Shrew. "Why'd you want to know?"

"I worked for her, that's why."

Despite the fact she looked no different from me, Shrew sneered at my rough striped dress and my stubbly head. "Yeah, I heard you made gowns for Madam H. Then you got beat up."

"Marta booted Rose and me out for no good reason. She

uses everyone to get ahead, then takes credit for their work. All she cares about is herself!"

"Yeah? Tell that to her sister."

"What sister?"

Shrew squirmed with delight at having this gossip to stir up. "Her sister Lila. Couple of years older than Marta. A teacher. Married—two little kids, just toddlers, and a baby on the way. Word came Lila was on a List for a work camp, and we all know what *that* means."

"Hard labor till you drop, or a one-way trip to this place. Ha, ha, ha!" laughed Hyena.

"Right," said Shrew. "So Marta says to Lila, 'You can't leave the kiddies; I'll go in your place.' Gave up a job at a nice dress salon, from what I've heard. Ends up here, works hard, lands on her feet as a prominent—who can blame her for getting ahead? I heard the whole story from a cousin who knows a girl who works for Mrs. Smith at the Department Store, so it's practically from the horse's mouth. Every word's true."

Marta had volunteered to come in her sister's place? She'd sacrificed her career and her freedom, in return for Birchwood? It gave a whole new twist to the question *What would Marta do?*

And then there was Carla.

"I still don't get why Carla did this to me," I later complained to Rose, taking the red ribbon out of my secret pocket-bag and letting it glide over my stiff fingers.

Rose said, "She's under a spell, of course, cast by a powerful enchanter in his eagle-nest lair many leagues away . . ."

And so another story began.

There were tons of possible answers—*because she was bored, because she's a brute, because she's jealous, because she can.* None of them (or all of them) made sense.

About a week after we came to the Washery, Carla showed up. I hid behind a row of drying shirts and watched as she stopped in the shelter of a wall to light a cigarette. I was terrified she'd spot me and come to add more bruises to the collection I already had.

I wanted to run and hide, like a fox going to ground, but I couldn't move.

Carla took a couple of drags on the cigarette, stubbed it against the wall, then dropped it on the ground and walked off. I waited till she was out of sight, then dodged through the washing to pick up the cigarette butt. Riches!

The next day Carla came back again. This time she was with a friend—just two guards smoking and chatting like any other normal pair of pals or workers on a cigarette break. Once again Carla dropped the cigarette stubs on the ground. Once again they'd barely been puffed. It couldn't be an accident that she was leaving valuable litter at the place I now worked. Was this her way of trying to make up for wrecking my hand and my chance of sewing her

158

beautiful clothes? Did she want to repair what she thought of as a friendship?

I hid the cigarettes in my secret under-dress pocket-bag until they were needed.

I meant to tell Rose about Carla.

"Guess what happened earlier," I began, the first time I spotted Carla smoking.

"Shh," she said. "I'm nearly at the end of the chapter . . ."

We were standing under a line of wet washing, not a book in sight. I waited. Finally Rose gave a little sigh and blinked.

"It was hard at first," she said. "Trying to remember it all."

"Remember what?"

"A storybook my mama read to me at bedtime when I was little."

"Lucky you," I said enviously. No one had told me stories at bedtime until Rose.

Rose tucked her arm in mine. "You don't realize it at the time — how much you take for granted. When They came to arrest my parents, Mama said she'd find me after the War. She will, won't she?"

It threw me to hear Rose less than confident. "*Of course* she will. You've got to hope, remember? The red ribbon — that's what it stands for." It didn't sound half as convincing when *I* said it.

"I wish you'd kept it on as a bandage," she said.

I was gruff. "I've got to get my hand working properly

159

again. Lying around with it in a sling being fed grapes is hardly an option here."

"It's better to let it heal slowly — that way you'll get full use back. You'll be able to sew again."

I had my doubts about that.

Rose made a new friend. He was a gardener. If Rose had come and told me she'd made friends with a dragon, I would have been no more surprised. And yet, not far from the drying ground, there was a patch of tilled soil called a garden.

It was weeded and watered by a Stripey so ancient he had to be at least fifty years old. I thought of him as a tortoise — slow, dull, and wrinkled. His legs were so bent there was almost room to push the laundry basket between them. His back was so rounded I could've balanced the basket on top.

This grizzled old wreck took a shine to Rose when she nipped over to admire the brave vegetables that were defying the odds to grow in Birchwood's ashy air. Apparently the guards liked fresh fruit and veggies. I suppose They had to have something to balance out all the cakes and wine they scarfed.

Tortoise's pride and joy was a stunted rose bush. Rose was honored — he allowed her close enough to sniff the perfume of its tiny blush-red buds. The two of them never spoke beyond her compliments and his wheezing. He touched his striped cap to her when she appeared, as if she really was a countess and he was her staff.

Rose reminisced. "Our head gardener used to compete with other estates as to who could grow the first green peas of the year. You should have seen the fuel bill, to heat the greenhouses in the walled garden."

I ignored her tall tales, eyed the veggies, and wished I could gobble the lot.

Summer's death rattle was a few dried-up birch leaves blowing between the blocks. There were no beautiful autumn colors. We went from clear skies to cold, endless gray. Gray skies, gray mood, gray washing. Then came the rain—gray floods of it, day after day after day. The first time we were on duty and it started to rain, we hoofed it to the lines to get the washing in. A passing guard saw us. She waved her arms and shouted, "Stupid bitches, leave it to dry!"

"B-but the rain?"

"You think you can change the weather just because you want an easy life doing nothing but sunbathing all day?" she screamed.

"It's not logical to leave it to dry in the rain," I muttered to Rose.

"If only we had little mice with umbrellas to stand along the washing line," she said wistfully.

I didn't like to argue with Rose's storybook logic any more than I dared argue with the guard, so we pinned the washing out again and watched it getting soaked. There were wool undershirts, ugly long johns, and woolen shorts—all gone gray in the wash. Oh, for the luxury of underwear of our own, instead of the daily indignity of doing without! I craved real clothes almost as much as I craved a full stomach.

We tried standing near a wall to get some shelter. Another guard yelled at us to stop loitering. We went back out onto the drying ground and stood in the rain, sucking our fingers to keep them warm.

"At least we're getting clean," said Rose through chattering teeth. She looked as gray as the washing, with little rosy fever spots on her cheeks.

By the time Hyena came out to call us in, the washing was wetter than ever, and we were both shivering. I tried to warm Rose by wrapping her in my arms and pulling her close to my own body.

She nestled in. "I can hear your heart beating," she said.

Rose kept me dreaming about dresses.

One morning, once she'd recovered from a sudden fit of coughing, she commanded, "Tell me a dress to go with this place."

"What do you mean? A dress to wear when we're watching the washing?"

"No — one inspired by the landscape, or an emotion you feel."

It seemed like a strange idea. Just the sort of storybook nonsense Rose would cook up. Still, I took the red ribbon out of my secret pocket-bag and let it twizzle around the fingers of my good hand. A dress appeared in my mind. I began to sketch it with words.

"That would have to be . . . let me see . . . a fine, soft gray wool-silk mix with a loose rolled collar, right up here, to the throat, and skirt all the way down to the feet. Long sleeves, with points from the wrist nearly to the floor. Metal weights in the hem, to keep everything trailing. Over the top, a mist of lace embroidered with silver drops. At the shoulders, a cloud of marabou feathers."

Rose was delighted. "Oh, Ella, when you say it, I can see it. You'll make that dress when we get our shop. Once we launch the autumn/winter collection, the clients will all swoon in their seats as soon as it's shown. We'll have so many orders we'll be turning customers away. 'So sorry, milady. Apologies, Your Highness. No more frocks for sale today!'"

She curtsied in her stripes and mismatched shoes. I had to laugh.

Then I looked out at the rain falling on free ground beyond the barbed wire. "Do you think the War will ever end? Will we really have a shop?"

Rose put a gentle kiss on my red ribbon. "Have a little hope, Ella. You never know when something good will happen."

About half an hour later, that's all it took.

I had a laundry basket perched on my bony excuse for a hip. I was lugging it back to the mangle room, walking in the shadow of the Washery wall, when—*whump!*—a giant sausage fell out of the sky and landed right on the pile of damp shirts.

163

I looked around. Nobody in sight. I heard the click of a window closing and looked up. Did somebody drop a sausage out by accident, or was it thrown to me? Either way, I was keeping it. I covered the sausage with clothes and hurried to catch up with Rose.

She laughed when I told her what had happened.

"A sausage fell out of the sky into the laundry basket? You couldn't make it up!"

"*You* could," I said. "And if it actually is from one of your stories, could you please imagine some potatoes and peas to go with it?"

Our food situation had gotten even worse with the onset of autumn. Instead of colored water with bits, we just got the water, murky with some sort of grit but no real ingredients. The guards were twitchier too.

We ate half the sausage straightaway and gave the other half to Tortoise. He came hobbling up to us later that day, tugged Rose's sleeve, and opened his clawed hands to show her three colorless mushrooms.

Rose leaned forward and took a deep breath of them. "*Mushrooms!* I'd forgotten they even existed."

Tortoise grunted and shoved them at her.

"For me?" By force of habit Rose looked around for witnesses. No guards or bosses were nearby. "Really?"

Tortoise tapped the side of his nose, showed a bare-gummed smile, and shuffled off.

We both stared at those mushrooms for a long minute, and then I couldn't stand it any longer.

"So can we flippin' eat them or what?"

"And how would you like them served, my dear?" Rose teased, cradling the mushrooms to her, like they were a brood of teeny-weeny babies. "With a cream sauce, on buttered toast? In a wild venison stew with herbed dumplings?"

"Just raw will do. I know what'll happen if we get back to the barrack to heat them by the stove there — you'll break them into fractions and share them all out."

"There aren't really enough for everyone, but do you think we *should* share?"

"No!"

We ate them raw, savoring each tiny nibble. We felt like queens at a feast.

Two days later, pegged between the rows of gray guard socks was a paper packet. Like a magician I disappeared it, to open later, in secret. When I did I had to borrow some of the Washery women's less toxic swear words.

Chocolate.

Gray-brown wartime chocolate, to be fair, but still *chocolate*! My fingers trembled as I broke off a square and put it on my tongue.

It's only when you've been without something that you truly appreciate how wonderful it is. That square of chocolate melted in my mouth like food of the gods. Birchwood melted away too, and I was back home . . . on my way home, at least, from school.

We — me and a bunch of school friends — had stopped

165

at the newsstand. They were all going straight for the sweets. I was counting my money and trying to decide between a fashion magazine and chocolate. I only had enough for one or the other. I remember looking at the chocolate and thinking how easy it would be to slip a bar up my sleeve without paying, without the twitchy hamster-woman at the till noticing a thing.

Was it stealing to take the chocolate from the washing line? Did I care?

What would Rose do?

Ask me who could've left it there, then break it into equal squares and share it with everybody and anybody. That's what Rose would do.

We used the chocolate paper to line Rose's shoes because her feet were going blue-gray with the cold. I bartered some of the chocolate for Girder's permission to let Rose sit near the barrack stove in the evening. Maybe that would stop her shivering. The rest we divided up and ate, morsel by morsel.

Rose said that in stories, things happened in threes. So a hero would be given three tasks on her quest, or there'd be three brothers going off on an adventure, that sort of thing. Sausage. Chocolate. The third gift wasn't edible. It was a card.

I'd seen things like it in the shops back home — beautiful

squares of embroidered silk spelling out birthday wishes, or true love. This card was tucked into a pair of gray underpants on the washing line, with the name ELLA on the envelope. It had a picture of two birds holding a heart between them. On the back, a penciled message: *Look out for me in the morning.*

All that evening we talked about the card. I had a friend! (An admirer?)

"A fairy godmother," said Rose, determined to turn it into a story.

Morning came, gray and drizzly. Rose woke me up with a tremendous bout of sneezing, followed by an equally energetic coughing session. Roll call was over quickly — only two hours, since nobody messed the counting up by dying halfway through. We hurried to the drying ground.

There was nobody there.

Disappointed, I plunged my hands into mounds of wet washing and began to pin. I was wrestling with a particularly obstinate pair of pajamas when I felt something warm behind me. A hand went over my mouth. A voice whispered, "Shhh."

I knew him straightaway. It was the faithful dog: Henrik.

"I've finally tracked you down!" Henrik said, flicking socks and long johns at me. He was taller and broader even than I remembered, and just as annoyingly friendly.

"What are you doing here?" I said. "You broke my sewing machine!"

"Is that all the thanks I get?"

"I was making a dress. I had to finish by hand, you interfering idiot."

Henrik laughed. "I should've remembered how passionate you are about all that sewing stuff. Aren't you glad to see me? Did you like the gifts?"

"That was *you*?"

"Who did you think it was?"

"I don't know." *Carla? The gardener? Some invisible fairy godmother?*

"You're welcome," he said sarcastically.

"What? Oh, thank you. Thank you very much."

"What happened to your hand? Is that why you're not sewing anymore?"

I really didn't know how to be around Henrik. He was nothing like the bookish boys at school, or the more tough-guy gangs I sometimes used to meet while walking home.

"Who are you?" I asked.

"Henrik! I told you."

"I know your name, but that's it."

"Oh, you want me to come home and meet your father, to ask permission to speak to you? Let me see . . . what would I tell him?"

"Tell *me* instead."

"OK, brief history. I left school last year. Got a job as a garage mechanic, going nowhere fast. Then there was the War. Obviously, thanks to my religion"—he tapped the yellow star sewn on his striped jacket—"I got on a List for this place. But I'm doing all right. In fact, I'm doing really well. Making a difference, which is great. As a general fixer-upper I get access to all sorts of different buildings in the camps. I can pass messages and news—"

"And organize sausages for strangers . . ."

"Plenty more where that came from. And anyway, you're not a stranger. We're friends, aren't we?"

I thought about the heart on the silk card and didn't know what to say.

We had reached the end of the washing line and the view out over free fields.

I felt Henrik behind me, keeping me sheltered from some of the cold wind.

He murmured, "Even on a bleak day, freedom's still a fine sight, isn't it?"

"Yeah, if you could forget the sentry boxes, the land mines, the dogs, and the three rows of fencing and barbed wire."

Softly: "True." Softer still: "What if you could?"

"Could what?"

"Forget the fences. The barriers. What if you could get free?"

"You mean . . . ?"

"Escape, my dear dressmaker. Escape!"

* * *

Henrik didn't say much more, just enough to tantalize. He pointed to a train slowly gathering speed as it left Birchwood to return to the outside world.

"They come in full, but they don't go back empty," he said.

"People get to leave?"

"Not people . . . officially. Things stolen from new arrivals. Thousands of crates and bales of goods get loaded on."

"Things from the Department Store?" I got a snapshot in my mind—glasses, shoes, and suitcases, piled high like treasure.

"Exactly. I've got friends in what they call the White Cap work squad—the prisoners who fumigate and pack all the bundles for transport. It may just be possible to arrange an escape that way."

Escape! Freedom! Home!

That night in the barrack block I hid under the bunk blanket with Rose. I was bursting with excitement as I told her about Henrik, without mentioning his talk of escape. I don't know why I veered away from that. Perhaps it was too precious an idea to share yet. Perhaps it was too dangerous.

Rose said Henrik was kind to give us food. Then she sneezed for the thousandth time that evening and fished in her sleeve for a scrap of cotton that passed for a hankie.

"I know a story about a magic handkerchief that turned

snot into fishes," she said, with a throat so sore her voice came out grated, like hard cheese.

"It'd be better to turn it into gold. Then we could buy a dress shop once the War's over."

"They could be *gold*fishes, I suppose. Hey, Ella, do you want to hear what happened during a flu epidemic one winter, when all the fishponds were frozen . . . ?"

And off she went, into story land—her own kind of escape.

The snuffling, sneezing, and wheezing were bad enough. What was worse was her cough, and the way she shivered all the time, even when she felt boiling hot to touch. We were all so undernourished that even the slightest health problem could be lethal.

I went to Bear at the Washery and told her to find Rose and me jobs indoors, out of the rain. The way things were going we wouldn't survive a winter without shelter.

Bear's little eyes got even smaller. I guessed that meant she was thinking.

"Getting a touch wet for you out there?" snickered her sidekick, Hyena. She could see water was literally running down my face from my sodden headscarf.

"Have you ever wondered what it would be like to drown?" I asked her sweetly.

Hyena slid behind Bear.

Bear was sometimes sleepy, sometimes grumpy, and

always slow. Eventually she made the connection between the handful of cigarette ends I was offering and the idea of me and Rose coming indoors. She took the cigarettes. Job done.

Next I went to Tortoise. He was hoeing his patch of garden in slow motion. I asked if he could spare any greens for Rose. I'd probably get shot if anyone found out—as would the gardener. Never mind that. Rose needed vitamins. Tortoise tottered off and cut me a few leaves from a cabbage. Not the whole thing—guards would notice that. I thanked him. He nodded, then cleared his throat. After all those weeks of silence it seemed he was finally going to speak. He had a ghost of a voice.

"If . . . *when* they come for me, look after my rose, will you?"

I looked at the stunted little bush sticking out of the veggie patch—more thorns than blooms. When it was warm he'd picked aphids off it by hand. Now that there were frosts in the morning, he'd wrapped the stems with straw to keep them snug.

I wasn't much into gardening. Still, there was something about the way Tortoise loved that patch of soil, despite all the gray ash that rained over Birchwood. I suppose he was nurturing his own bud of hope. I thought of Grandad, and how much he'd hate to leave everything he knew and loved.

Grandad had his own little habits, such as making me paper boats from cigarette papers, or humming a few warning notes when coming through a door, or swinging his walking stick *just so* every second step he took along the pavement. Surely they couldn't put *him* on a List? What had he ever done to anyone, except bore them pantsless going on about horse-racing results?

I nodded to Tortoise.

"I will. I promise."

Two days later the gardener was plucked out of line at roll call. His number was on the worst List of all: people surplus to requirements. We weren't there—the men had their roll call in an entirely different part of camp from the women. Even so, I could imagine him shuffling along like a tortoise, prodded by guards with their rifle butts.

When I told Rose, she ran out of the Washery and straight to the little garden, where she promptly pulled every single rose bloom off the branches, scattering the petals into the ashy wind.

"I hate Them! Hate Them! *Hate* Them! They don't deserve to have any beauty!" she cried savagely. If she hadn't been crippled by a sudden attack of coughing, she might have ripped that bush up by the roots.

I hustled her away before any guards came. It was only later, in the prickling straw of the barrack bunk, that I realized Tortoise hadn't just been talking about flowers when he said, *Look after my rose.* The human Rose was very still at my side. Too still. I touched my hand to her chest to find a heartbeat . . . and felt only ribs. In a panic, I leaned closer. I was rewarded with a wisp of breath on my cheek. A rose asleep in a world of thorns.

I sighed at such a romantic image. Rose's fairy-tale fancies were contagious.

Indoors was warmer, which was something. It was worse in other ways, though. Hot, claustrophobic, and cripplingly hard work.

How soon can we escape? was my sole thought as I plunged my bare arms into the scalding heat of a washtub. *How soon can we escape?* as I rubbed stinky socks and sweaty shirts on a washboard. *How soon can we escape?* while I rinsed off the stinging soap in biting cold water.

The other Washery workers were bullies, plain and simple. They banged laundry trolleys against our bare legs. They stole our blocks of soap, kicking them around the wet stone floor like a hockey puck. Then one of them, a broad-shouldered bull of a woman, *accidentally* jostled me as I carried my soup-water, making it slop over the tin. She was a Birchwood veteran. One of the low numbers who'd been in the camp for several years. She was so bold she actually smoked cigarettes, instead of using them for barter.

It wasn't the first time she'd had a go at me. I felt warm liquid splash on my dress and run down my leg.

"Watch what you're doing!" I snapped.

"You shouldn't get in my way," bellowed Bull.

"Ha, ha, ha, ha, ha!" laughed Hyena, as Bear looked on.

"I wasn't in your way," I shouted at Bull-woman. "You pushed me."

"It was an accident," said Rose. "Here, you can share mine."

"It was deliberate!" I cried. "*She* should give me *her* soup."

Bull's nose wrinkled. She gave a funny toss of her head, stamped her feet, then reached out and swiped Rose's soup tin out of her hand.

"Ha, ha, ha, ha, ha!" came Hyena's cry.

"Now whose soup will you share?" taunted Bull.

I was in such a fury I smashed my tin around her face, then head-butted her in the stomach. Down she went, and I kicked her for good measure. I only got away with it because she hadn't been expecting the attack . . . and because no guards noticed. I looked around, fists clenched, to see if anyone else wanted a turn.

They all shrank away. Hyena stopped cackling. I picked up Bull's bowl and went to get it filled for myself.

Rose was horrified, so I said I was sorry. I wasn't. Not one minuscule bit. Fighting back had been glorious. Later, as I was pounding, scrubbing, swishing, squeezing, I imagined I had Hyena in my hands instead of laundry.

We weren't bullied anymore.

"We do what we can to survive," I told Rose, trying to justify my attack. "We can't let people see us as weak."

She sighed. "I know. But . . . how much will you toughen up before you start being like Them?"

"You're comparing me to the *guards*? I'm nothing like Them! They signed up for this work! I got dragged off the street on my way home from school! They get decent beds and food and treats from the Department Store. I get excited if there's a carrot top floating in my soup-water at supper! They've got whips and dogs and guns and gas chambers and—"

"I didn't mean you're the same," Rose interrupted. "But it does remind me of a story, you know. About mice who got guns and learned how to use them against the cats . . ."

"Guns!" said Henrik, next time I met him. "If we could get our hands on more *guns*, we'd have a much better chance against the guards."

He and I were outside, standing close together as protection from the bitter winter winds. I was watching red ribbons of fire lighting the sky above the chimneys. I'd given up pretending those chimneys didn't exist. When guards threatened to "send you to the gas" for the slightest minor misdemeanor, it was pointless to pretend I wasn't living in a world where people were poisoned then burned by the thousands. By the tens of thousands. Hundreds of thousands maybe.

Henrik sensed my mood. He put his arm around my bony shoulders. I said I hoped the War would be over soon.

"Hope!" He spat the word out. "It's not *hope* we need, Ella, you fluff-ball. It's *action*—proof we're not victims, that we won't go quietly to our fate, like sheep to the slaughter! Something's planned soon . . . you'll see. An uprising! Us against Them! Glory and liberty!"

I reported this back to Rose. "Glory and liberty, Rose! An *uprising!*"

Rose sniffed — runny nose or disapproval? "Heroism's all well and good until guts are spilled. What use is a flag or fancy words when you're a good-looking corpse?"

"Henrik's not afraid. He's brave."

"Are courage and desperation enough against machine guns?"

"Better than doing *nothing at all*," I snapped. "Telling stories about what we'll be after the War, stories that can't ever come true if we don't survive this place!"

Rose shivered. "You're right," she said quietly, too tired, it seemed, to fight.

When the uprising started, we were both up to our elbows in soap suds and greasy clothes. A great *BOOM* shook Birchwood. We steadied ourselves against the washtubs in shock.

"What was that?" we all asked, but no one could answer. Bear stomped off to find out more. Next we heard machine-gun fire and pistol shots. Dogs were going crazy. My heart beat faster than a speeding train. Was this it? Was this the glory and liberty Henrik had been on about?

I waited for him to come bursting into the Washery, with some flag waving behind him and a brass band playing marching music. That's how it would be in a film.

The reality?

It was an uprising by the work gangs over by the gas chambers—that much was true—but a failed one. Shrew reported rumors of explosives smuggled into Birchwood to blow up the gas chambers. Stripeys turning on guards. Guards gunning down Stripeys. By nightfall the rebellion was quashed. Dead. Before long all but one of the chimneys of Birchwood were smoking again and a gray ash blew over us all.

I felt twisted inside, worrying that Henrik had been caught up in it.

Then, relief. I received a smuggled note at the Washery.
Our time will come soon. Wash and wait X

It wouldn't be soon enough for Rose. From the corner of my eye I saw her struggling to heave wet clothes from her tub. She had one shirt gripped in the giant wooden laundry tongs . . . and couldn't lift it. She caught a sock, and she still couldn't lift it. Before I could reach her she was flat on the floor, as limp as the wet sock beside her.

"Rose . . . Rosalind, it's me, Ella."

I leaned over the bed and smoothed little strands of hair from her brow.

"Shh, don't try and talk yet," I murmured.

Her breath rasped. "Ella." That's all she managed. Her eyes turned from side to side then widened in horror.

"I'm so, so sorry, Rose, I had to bring you here. You were unconscious for hours, then delirious and feverish. I hid you at the barrack block for two days. Girder said you might be contagious. There was nothing else to do."

A gasp turned into a cough. Her whole body shook. I held her close — a precious bundle of bones. It was awful to be so helpless. Harder still was the horror the Hospital inspired in me. How could anyone possibly *live* in this place, let alone recover from illness or injuries? It was more like a morgue than a hospital. Everyone was squished into rotten tiered bunks like stinking sardines in a tin. No toilets. No bedpans. Stripeys with nurses' armbands checked who was still breathing and who could be hauled out to make room for new arrivals.

"Here, I brought breakfast." I hadn't seen any sign of food in the Hospital block. Most of the so-called patients were too ill to feed themselves, even if there had been enough staff to dole food out . . . or enough food to sustain life. The only nurse who'd come close was a waddling duck of a woman with a grubby apron over her prison stripes. Her job seemed to consist of writing patients' numbers on a List. So far Rose's number wasn't on it.

I'd already begged this Nurse Duck to treat Rose's fever. She'd just looked at me as if to say, *What with?*

"This place, it's just for a day or two," I reassured Rose.

"Till you're better and Girder says you can come back to the barrack block, and Bear says you can work at the Washery again. Here—do you think you can eat a bit? There's bread, margarine, and *this*!"

With a flourish I produced a wizened apple—a princely gift from Henrik.

Rose stared at it as if she'd forgotten what an apple was. Then she smiled a weak smile. "Did I ever tell you about the time—?"

"No stories, idiot! Save your strength."

Rose took the apple and sniffed in its scent. "It reminds me of a tree," she said. "In the City of Light . . . the park . . . an apple tree. Just one—branches spilling blossoms everywhere in spring."

She spread her fingers and I almost saw those blossom petals fall.

"If anything happens . . ." she continued.

"Nothing's going to happen!"

"If anything happens, we'll meet there, at the park, under the tree, the same day we met at the sewing room."

I couldn't comprehend what she was saying. "We'll go together, Rose, you and me."

She nodded, but that set off a spasm of coughs again. When she finally caught her breath, her face was glistening with sweat.

I'd no idea how she even knew the date we were sent to the Upper Tailoring Studio. The last calendar date I remembered was the last day I came home from school.

But Rose remembered, and made me repeat to her the date we'd meet at that park, at that tree.

"You won't forget? You'll be there?" she wheezed.

"We'll both be there."

"Of course we will. But if we get separated, go to the tree and wait for me. Remember — we'll tie the red ribbon to a branch to celebrate meeting again. Promise me we'll meet at the tree, Ella. On that day. Promise . . ."

"I promise."

Rose sank down into my arms. Her eyes closed. I felt her cheeks — so hot! How gray she looked in the dim light of the Hospital, my little Squirrel.

"I have to go now, Rose. Try to eat."

"I will," she whispered. "I'm just not so hungry right now. I'll be better tomorrow."

"Get stronger."

Rose nodded weakly, then turned away.

I wanted to wail and throw things and run at the barbed-wire barrier in a rage. Instead I had to think of a way to get medicine in a world where one aspirin was more precious than a nugget of gold.

"You again!"

I stood in the doorway of the sewing workshop. It was all painfully familiar, although not quite as buzzing as I remembered. Francine, Shona, Brigid, and others smiled hello. They mouthed, *Hey, Ella, how are you? How's Rose?* I tried not to look at Betty, my grandma's sewing machine, but there it was, at my old table, with some other Stripey using it. Another woman was at Rose's old spot too, ironing. How quickly we'd been replaced.

My fingers twitched to be handling fabric again. I was getting normal movement back in my injured hand. I could hold a spoonful of soup-water without spilling it. I could probably manage Betty with practice.

"The answer's no," came Marta's voice.

"You don't even know what I'm going to ask!"

"And still the answer's no."

I kept my temper. Since that one short note—*Wash and wait*—I'd had no word from Henrik, so Marta was my next best hope. Which meant pretending to be humble. I had the red ribbon hidden in one hand. I clutched it for courage.

"Please—listen. It's not for me, it's for Rose. She's sick."

"Then she should be in the Hospital."

"She is."

That made Marta pause. Just saying the word *Hospital* had that effect in Birchwood. Usually only lost causes went to the Hospital.

"Then there's nothing I can do."

"Of course there is, if you wanted to! You're a prominent. You send Shona to shop at the Department Store almost every day. I've seen that place—I *know* they'll have something to help with Rose's fever, or vitamins at least . . . food with more goodness than the watery junk we all get."

"So what if I could help? Why should I?"

182

I looked her square in the eyes. "Because you're a human being, the same as the rest of us. I know about your sister Lila, how you saved her."

Marta's eyes blazed. "Shut up! *Shut up!* You know *nothing!*"

Marta grabbed my arm and pulled me next door into the empty fitting room. The thud when I was shoved against the wall made the bobbles on the lampshade tremble. The tin fell from her pocket and scattered pins everywhere. Neither of us moved to pick them up.

"Don't ever mention my sister again, you understand?"

"But it was a good thing you did —"

"*Good?* I ended up in *here.* What's good about that? What else did you hear about me?"

"Nothing. Just the sacrifice you made to keep her safe."

Marta's grip on me tightened. "So you don't know about how I went to the fashion house where I worked — one of the very best places, it was — to ask for advance payment on my wages. Just enough to pay to get my family hidden away safely. These people who'd known me for *five years,* who'd watched me work my fingers to the bone for them six or seven days a week — late nights, no overtime, since I was a thirteen-year-old apprentice — these people looked down their noses at me and said, *We can't possibly do that.* And I know what they were thinking: that I must be *tainted* if my family was at risk of being deported."

"That's —"

"Shut up!"

Marta let go of me. She paced up and down the fitting-room floor, like a shark that can never stop swimming.

"The next day," she said, in a low furious voice, "the very next day I received formal notice that I was being sacked. Because way back somewhere in my family history there's someone of the *wrong* ancestry. So, yes, I said I'd go in my sister's place to some so-called *work camp*. I was stronger, right? Fitter for work. That seemed to suit the authorities. Next stop—Birchwood. Two weeks later They put my sister on a new List anyway. And not just Lila. Her children, her husband, our parents, our aunts, uncles, cousins, in-laws—*everyone*, smoke and ashes. Much good my noble sacrifice was. I'm the only one still alive now, so don't talk to me about *good*. If you know what's *good* for you, you'll follow my example and forget about anything to do with family or friends. The only thing that matters is to *survive*. I'll tell you this, little schoolgirl—I'm going out of this place on my own two feet, not up one of those chimneys!"

Marta finally stopped pacing. She was breathing heavily. Was this a good time to smash the lamp over her head?

I rubbed my bruised arm. "It stinks, how you were treated."

"Damn right it stinks."

"So why treat other people the same way?"

"Haven't you figured it out yet? Nothing more inhuman than a human being. Not just the rulers and politicians . . . all the selfish evil of everyday people, too. Isn't this place

184

proof enough?" She swept her arms out to include the whole of the Birchwood universe.

What would Rose say?

Something nice.

"It's also human nature to *help*, Marta. To sacrifice."

"Yeah? Well, I'm not going to *sacrifice* any more of my precious time helping you. Get out."

We stared at each other for the longest time, in mutual hatred. Then I shrugged.

"You know something, Marta? I feel sorry for you."

"What?"

"You heard me."

"You feel sorry for *me*? I'm an important person here! You're, what, working in the Washery? How dare you feel sorry for me?"

I turned away in disgust.

Marta wasn't finished. "Come back here when I'm talking to you! Come here!"

I walked out. I might have knocked over the lamp as I left. The sound of it smashing gave me a savage burst of satisfaction. But even as the lamp broke and the door slammed shut, I turned the anger against myself—how could all my noble talk possibly persuade Marta when I wasn't even convinced myself?

Expecting Marta to help had been crazy, but my next plan was plain suicidal. There was only one other person I could think of to ask.

I dodged between barracks with my head down—just another Stripey scuttling about like a rat. I came to the right entrance. Pushed it open. Crept down the corridor to the right door. Knocked—no louder than a fly settling on wood. No reply. I knocked more loudly.

Carla had been sitting on her bed, reading letters, by the look of it. Handwritten sheets were scattered on the patchwork quilt. She had a mug of hot chocolate steaming by the bed and a half-eaten packet of cookies open on the chest of drawers, next to the photo of her in a meadow with Rudi the farm dog. No sign of her roommate, Grazyna the Bone-Grinder, thank god.

Carla smelled of shampoo and Blue Evening perfume. Her eyes were red-rimmed. At first I thought she'd slam the door in my face. That she'd shout to raise the alarm. That I'd be torn apart like a hunted fox if the other guards knew I was here.

Instead she rubbed her eyes and looked at the floor. "You'd better come in."

Seeing her collection of family photos gave me a sharp pain in my chest and a big lump in my throat. It was taking more and more effort to imagine myself back in Grandma's sewing room, watching her slippered foot go up and down on the treadle of Betty the sewing machine . . . her ringed fingers guiding fabric under the needle . . . her stool creaking as she leaned in to snip thread.

I had to get home.

* * *

Carla mumbled, "Things aren't so good anymore. Did you hear? Some prisoners murdered some guards and blew up . . . necessary buildings. It's scary. I don't know how long we'll go on."

I was standing in front of her, my dress stained with sudsy water, hands raw from scrubbing long johns, and bones showing from too little food . . . and all Carla could think about was how scared *she* was.

She flicked a quick look at my face, then down to my hand. The one she'd smashed under her boot.

"It's . . . it's a shame you're not sewing anymore," she said. "You really were the best seamstress at that place. You should open a shop after the War, like Madam said. I'll be a customer. I'll pay, of course!"

Her optimism was hard and forced.

"I need medicine and vitamins," I said.

"Are you OK? Are you sick?"

"Not for me. For a friend."

Carla's pig-eyes narrowed. *"Her?"* She knew who I meant. She said it like an accusation.

I nodded.

She turned abruptly and went to straighten her photos. I waited. For help, for another beating.

"There's no point," she said eventually.

"No point what?"

187

"No point wasting medicine on sick people. You ought to look after yourself. It won't be long now. Half a year, maybe sooner, and the War will be over. You'll put in a good word for me, won't you?" She looked up at me through her eyelashes. "You'll let everybody know that I was never cruel like the others? I hate this place as much as you do, you know. After the War we'll forget about it, as if it never existed. We'll get to go home. First thing I'm going to do is take Pippa to the meadow at the farm. I'll pick flowers in spring and go shopping. . . ."

Carla moved to the bed. She wallowed there, flipping the pages of *Fashion Forecast*, which was open on her pillow.

I could barely speak, the lump of fury in my throat was so hot and hard. Had this pig-brained girl genuinely forgotten what a brute she'd been? My hands made fists. My palms were burning as my nails dug in. I swallowed my pride.

"You have to help me," I begged. "After all the beautiful things I made for you . . ."

Carla's gentle mood exploded into fury. "I don't have to do *anything*. I'm a guard here and you're . . . you're not even a *person*. You shouldn't even be in the same room as me, or breathing the same air. Look at you — a crawling bug, spreading disease. You should be crushed. You're disgusting! Get out! *Get out!*"

As I ran back to the Washery, the air was stained with gray cinders. Outside office blocks, guards were emptying filing cabinets and burning papers. They were destroying evidence of all the Birchwood bureaucracy.

It was hard to find time to get to the Hospital. The Washery was overloaded with dirty laundry. The drains were overloaded too. For once my wooden shoes didn't seem so stupid—the thick soles kept me above the water that sloshed on the Washery floor. The only time I took my shoes off was at night, when I used them as a pillow. And the time I threatened to wallop Shrew with a shoe when I caught her trying to steal my bread portion.

When I finally did get to see Rose, she was half propped up on the bed and awake.

"Hey—you've got a bit of color," I said. "Must've been the magic apple."

Rose reached up for a kiss. "It was delicious, absolutely delicious."

I sighed. "You didn't eat the apple, did you?"

"Not exactly . . . There was a girl in here with both legs crushed after an accident in the quarry. I gave it to her. She'd been a fashion model before the War—can you believe that?—in the City of Light! You should have heard her talk about all the glamorous gowns, and heels as high as skyscrapers! She said the models all lived off champagne and cigarettes, to keep thin."

"No need for that diet here," I grouched. Rose was getting so slight I could see every bone under her skin. I leaned in close. "Guess what? I've got a present for you!"

189

Rose brightened for a moment. "What is it? An elephant?"

"An elephant? Why on earth would I bring you an *elephant?*"

"So we could go for rides! Not an elephant, then." She pretended to think. "I know — a pony."

"No."

"Shame. A bicycle?"

"No!"

"A balloon? A birdcage? A . . . book? Is it really a book? One I can actually touch and read?"

"Better than that," I said, sliding a package out from my hidden pocket. "Look!"

Rose hoisted herself up onto one elbow. Gently she touched all the treats I'd brought, folded inside sheets of an old edition of *Fashion Forecast*. There were a few vitamin pills, a precious little hoard of aspirin tablets, and two sugar lumps. Also, half a packet of cookies.

From the way her face fell, I could tell a book would've excited her more.

"Where did you get all this?" she asked.

"A fairy godmother," I replied sarcastically.

"Really?"

"Of course not! I did some asking around. Got these as a favor."

"They're like jewels in a treasure chest." She folded the paper and pushed the packet back at me. "You should keep them. You're working, while I'm just lying here. No point feeding me up."

Suddenly furious, I whispered as loudly as I dared, "Listen, when I give you things, it's not for the fun of it, all right? This isn't a game or a story. It's about doing whatever we can to stay *alive*. Don't you want that?"

My anger shocked her. Before she could answer, she was overtaken by a series of bubbling coughs. Once the shudders had subsided, she seized my hand and croaked, "Of *course* I want to live! Ella, I can't bear the idea that in one second all the thoughts in my head could go flying out with nowhere to roost. I haven't forgotten our plan. We'll still open our shop when the War is over."

"You'd better believe it," I said, swallowing anger down into an empty stomach. "Dresses and books and cakes in the City of Light, the red ribbon on the apple tree, it's all going to happen. No barbed wire, no roll calls, no Lists, no guards, no chimneys. Can you *imagine*?"

"You're asking *me* to imagine now?"

"Don't be snarky! Promise me you'll get better."

I hugged her close. She trembled in my arms.

"I promise," she whispered faintly.

I took the red ribbon from my pocket-bag and pressed it into Rose's hand.

"It's so warm," she murmured. "And it's yours. You need it. Take it back. . . ."

"Rubbish. It's yours now. *You* can tie it on the tree in the City of Light when we go there."

Nurse Duck came flapping between the beds, looking ready to peck at me for staying too long.

191

I kissed Rose quickly and whispered, "Sorry, I have to get back to the Washery. . . .You know how it is."

She smiled, even though she was already drifting away. "Good night, Ella."

"Good night, Rose."

The miracle package was from Carla. It had been delivered to Girder by a Stripey, with the message that I was to get it whole, no pilfering. That annoyed Girder. To be fair, most things annoyed Girder. I couldn't worry about that. I could help Rose, giving her all the medicine and sugar. Well, I did eat *one* of the lumps of sugar. I was ravenous, and it would maybe rot Rose's teeth if she ate it all. What I didn't give her, what I didn't even mention, was the ring.

Not a plain band of wedding gold like the one squeezing my grandma's plump finger. Not a cheap tin ring won at a fair, with a "jewel" made of a sliver of mirror. This was a twinkling stone set in a circle of gold. When no one was looking, I slipped it on my finger and turned it from side to side.

It was just very fancy glass that twinkled like a diamond. Never mind that. Instead of a red ribbon, I had a ring to scatter light in the darkness. If I ever got out of here, if the War ever ended and I got to the City of Light, I would sell this ring to pay for the start of my dress-shop dream.

Out in the real world it had all seemed more obvious: who was a friend, who was an enemy. You could laugh, joke, talk, and do stuff with friends outside, but nobody had to show what they were really like. Not till they were dumped in Birchwood and stripped.

Without everyday clothes there was nothing to hide behind. Everybody had to be who they truly were, in a big muddled-up mess of everythingness — me included. Without proper clothes we couldn't dress up in a role. We couldn't put on glamorous gowns and say, *Darling, I'm rich and beautiful.* We couldn't button up high collars and announce ourselves as schoolteachers. No badges, hats, uniforms. No masks. We just had to be ourselves. We had to somehow hold on to what it meant to be a real person, not an animal.

How could I do that, surrounded by sharks and bulls and snakes? The mouse and butterfly types had long gone up the chimneys. My own dear Squirrel was hanging on — barely. And me? A fox that fed my family, or a fox that killed the farmer's chickens?

If I was a good person I'd've given Rose *all* the sugar. If I was a proper villain I'd've kept the whole lot for myself.

I was working a night shift at the scrubbing board when Henrik came bounding up like a dog who's just spotted a wonderful stick to carry.

"Ella! Thank god — I thought I wouldn't find you!"

"Henrik, you shouldn't be here."

"Shh, there isn't much time. Listen . . . it's happening!"

"What? Now? Tonight?"

"Tomorrow morning, just after roll call. Everything's been

chaotic after the uprising failed, but our contacts, timings, civilian clothes . . . everything's in place."

"Henrik, that's amazing! I can't believe it! Wait until I tell Rose—"

He grabbed my arm, quite roughly. I wish people would stop doing that. "You can't tell anyone, you goose. We can't risk a leak."

"Rose's hardly a spy. She's coming with us."

He let go of my arm abruptly. "That's just it, Ella. The plan is specific. There's only room for the two of us. Just the two of us, you understand?"

"Rose is only little, she wouldn't take up extra room. She won't be missed so much now she's at the Hospital."

"The *Hospital?* What's wrong with her?"

"Nothing getting out of this place wouldn't cure. She's got a chest infection."

"So she coughs?"

"Well, yes, a bit, but—"

"Ella, it's too dangerous. We're going to have to hide for hours in complete silence. One cough could blow our cover. Even if Rose can keep quiet, she's still got to pass as a normal civilian once we're in public again. We can't have anyone suspecting we're thin and pale because we've just escaped from this death factory!"

"With the right clothes, a hat, a bit of makeup . . ."

Henrik shook his head. "I'm sorry, Ella. Truly I am. I wish I could help everyone escape. That's what the uprising should've done. Those explosions, that was supposed to start everything off. The guards had too many machine guns. So, now we have to concentrate on getting ourselves out. As soon as we're free we'll go straight to one of the liberating armies. We'll be back here at the head of a convoy of tanks, with bomber planes flying overhead! We'll be the ones watching the guards cringe in fear, running for their lives!" There in the steam-filled washroom, Henrik mimed a silent machine-gun sweep.

It was a sweet, sweet image. I'd happily gun the lot of them down and bomb the whole of Birchwood to smithereens — *crash, bang, wallop!*

"This is your chance, Ella," Henrik said.

"But you swear we'll be back for Rose? That she'll only have to last until we liberate everyone?"

Henrik looked me straight in the eye. "Cross my heart, hope to die."

I barely slept that night. I was imagining what it would be like to walk free in a field. To stand under the stars without cringing. To wear normal clothes again. To be a person, not a Stripey.

We'd drink running water. Eat real bread. Maybe even sleep in beds. It was too exciting! We'd tell the world what was going on. They'd all rise up and rush to save the day, with Henrik on his tank and me waving a flag, or something heroic like that. Rose would come running to meet us, waving a flag too, or the red ribbon more likely.

Rose is too sick to run, said a niggle in my head.

But in my fantasy Rose jumped up on the tank and we trundled off across the fields to where the City of Light glowed like a diamond. Somehow we got dressed in amazing clothes along the way. We hopped off our tank and tied the red ribbon to the City of Light apple tree. . . .

Rose won't last that long without you, said the niggle.

It won't be long, I argued. *A few weeks at most before the liberators can get here.*

Rose was so selfless she'd be the first person to tell me to seize the chance and go, I was sure of it. Absolutely sure.

But the niggle kept on at me. Rose would need more than hope to survive until we came back for her. Fine, I told the niggle, I'd give Rose more than hope. She wasn't the only selfless one. I'd *buy* her a fighting chance.

When the whistles blew and the bosses began to shout at four thirty in the morning, I was ready. Alert, eager, and determined. In the general scramble for roll call, I sprinted between the blocks to the Hospital. There was time to say good-bye to Rose. To explain why I was going.

Except the door was locked.

I tapped on the window by the door. A face appeared. Nurse Duck. I pointed at the door. Her expression was blank. I mimed needing to get in. Still blank.

I fished two battered cigarettes out of my headscarf. "These are yours if you let me see Rose," I whispered.

Duck's face disappeared, then popped up again at a different window. With a bit of pushing, the window eased

196

open a fraction. I pressed up close. My breath was an icy cloud.

Duck shook her head. "The door's locked."

"I know! So open it."

"I can't."

I looked around again. There wasn't *time* for this! "Then tell her to come here, will you?"

Duck shook her head more vigorously this time. "Not going to happen."

"Will you at least take her a message? Tell her . . ." Tell her what? "Oh, stuff it. Here . . ."

Glancing around, I reached inside my dress, where I'd stitched my secret cloth pocket-bag. Carefully I took out a square of paper—another sheet from *Fashion Forecast*. On one side it had an ad for Blue Evening perfume, on the other an illustration of a gray wool coat. Duck watched me unfold the paper. Gold and glass glinted. My ring. My dream of a dress shop. My hope.

"Take this. It's all I've got left. Organize Rose medicine, buy her vitamins, food, blankets, whatever you can. Only, look after her till I come back, will you? Promise me you'll look . . ."

A pale hand reached out, snatched the treasure and withdrew. Then the window slammed shut.

Roll call always felt like forever. Now it was an infinity of waiting.

As soon as the whistles blew and groups scattered to

work, I was running too—off to the rendezvous point. Henrik ran up alongside me—my own eager dog.

"Follow me, a few paces behind," he said in a low voice. "Keep your eyes down."

He saw me hesitate and paused long enough to put two hands on my shoulders. "Look at me, Ella. Look at me! You're doing the right thing, you know that? Together we can make it."

"Together," I echoed.

He turned and moved away.

It was excruciating to go through Birchwood behind Henrik, as though nothing was out of the ordinary. All the time I thought of Rose and how much food and medicine that ring would buy. Enough to keep her well until I was back with an army as a glorious liberator! Then a horrible thought hit me. Of course Duck would keep it. She'd be mad not to. Marta would laugh her head off if she ever found out. She always said being soft was stupid, and she was right. *Stupid, stupid, stupid.*

We made it to a lightless hut where Henrik had hidden bundles of civilian clothes.

"Here, change quickly," he said. "We have to be ready for the next stage." He grinned. "Don't worry, I won't look."

I blushed in the dark. I'd barely been *alone* all the time I was in Birchwood. There were always people everywhere— women at work, women on roll call, guards and bosses . . . and Rose. Always Rose.

Henrik turned his back to me and began to button a gray cardigan over his shirt. I pulled my striped dress off and felt in the darkness for the normal clothes. They were poor quality. A thin wool skirt, cotton blouse, and threadbare sweater. The shoes were too small, with a squat, square heel. Even Grandma would've called them frumpy. But they were fine. Better than fine.

"I feel like a real person again," I whispered.

Henrik smiled down at me in the shadows. "You've always been real, right from that first time you told me, 'I'm Ella, I sew!' Now you look great. Just the sort of girl I need at my side . . ."

He leaned closer as footsteps passed the hut. I felt his breath on my face. Way off in the distance I heard a train whistle. My ride to freedom.

And so we smuggled ourselves out of Birchwood, avoiding the guards, the dogs, the machine guns, the barbed wire, the land mines. We hid among boxes and bundles of clothes loaded from the Department Store, then we jumped out at a station, bought tickets with some money Henrik had, and sat in a proper passenger train, on seats, as real people. Every mile of track took us toward freedom and closer to the end of the War. We joined the army of liberators. We sang songs of victory, wore patriotic medals, and we were heroes. We came back. We found Rose. We were happy.

That's what would have happened if I was telling a story.

* * *

I'd like to think Henrik got away all right. He wasn't dragged out to the gallows at roll call, to be executed like other Stripeys who'd been caught trying to escape. No gray cardigan clotted with blood and bullet holes was brought back to the camp to be pulped in the Rag Shed. I know. I went there to ask.

I stayed for Rose.

All day long in the Washery my hands were shaking. I heard a train whistle and hoped it meant the escape had worked. I heard dogs barking and people shouting. Mostly I just heard my own heart singing. I was filled with a kind of wild joy. I'd stayed! Yes, I was back to being a Stripey. Yes, I was still bound by barbed-wire fences. Somehow that didn't matter.

No one knew I'd been planning to go, so they just thought I was giddy for no reason. Hardly. In my mind I was seeing Rose's face light up when I arrived after evening roll call. Just twelve more hours to wait and work.

Long johns swished in the tub . . . and I carpeted our dress shop. Undershirts swirled in the suds . . . and I hung the curtains, polished glass lamps, and threaded the needle of my imaginary sewing machine. The sun sank into a gray mist and I was ordering cream buns from the cake shop next door. Picking sprigs of blossoms from the apple tree

200

in the park opposite. Shooing the last of the customers out of the shop.

Then roll call. Longer than ever. Shouting. Barking. Counting. Recounting.

The whistle blew. I ran, with hundreds of Stripeys running all around me under cold slices of light.

I ran, and then I stopped running.

This was the Hospital all right, so why was the door open? The windows too?

I crept inside. The beds were empty. There was filth and rubbish everywhere. Water sloshed as two skeletal Stripeys mopped the floor, just wetting the dirt and spreading it to different corners.

I almost couldn't speak.

"What happened here?"

The nearest Stripey looked up from her bucket, then looked down again. Then she answered in a dull voice, "What does it look like? Everyone in here was on a List."

"A List? Nobody said anything about that! How many did they take?"

Splosh went the mop in the gray water. "Didn't you hear me? *Everyone* was on the List. Patients, nurses, the lot. This place is empty. They're all gone."

I walked through the water and the muck to Rose's bunk. Her threadbare blanket had been dragged off the straw and onto the floor. Her crumpled headscarf was the only thing left on the bed.

"Gone?" My voice was a squeak. "Gone where?"

Slap went the mop on the floor. The Stripey's eyes flicked to one of the windows where flames gave the sky an unnatural sunset.

When I looked down I saw that Rose herself had given up. There it was, sodden with water and grime: the limp, red ribbon.

White

Wind, clouds, and ground remained. No birds sang. All leaves fell. The birch trees of Birchwood were naked and cold, like me under my striped dress.

The next morning I struggled out of a dream that Rose was dead.

A voice was calling from far, far away. "Wake up, wake up! Roll call!"

That didn't sound right. How could there be roll call when the world had stopped turning?

"Go away," I growled when someone shook me.

"Girder will kill you if you don't get up!"

"Let her."

"Oh, leave her," said someone else. "She was in a right foul mood last night."

Yes, leave me, I thought.

They left me. I stayed curled up in a ball, like a hedgehog. I must have dozed off again because this time I dreamed Rose was alive. Her hand was in mine. *Get up, lazybones,* she murmured in my ear.

"Let me sleep. . . ." I mumbled.

Sleep later. Get up now. Come on, I'll help you. Legs over the side of the bunk . . . that's right. Jump down. Don't forget your shoes.

"It's still dark, Rose. Can't we have a lie-in?"

Later, silly. Run now. That's it, take my hand. . . .Quickly now, the whistles are blowing.

"Rosalind, I missed you. I thought you'd gone."

I'm right here. I always will be.

"I didn't leave you. I couldn't leave without you."

I know, dearest, I know. Keep running.

She pulled me through the icy morning air, into the herd of mindless zebras. Together we made it to roll call.

"The chimneys are smoking," I whispered.

Don't look at them, Rose whispered back. *Just think of yourself. You're alive. You breathe. You think. You feel.*

After the first three hours I didn't feel the cold. I just felt Rose's hand in mine. I turned to tell her about the dream I'd had, where she was dead and I was alone. She wasn't there. Inside my frozen fingers, I had the red ribbon.

Don't go, don't go, don't go, I cried inside.

Rose was already gone. Somewhere in the icy air was her last breath. If I breathed in, would I taste it?

A whistle blew and left me standing, alone under a grim sunrise. Flakes of gray ash snowed down, oh so soft. Of all the horrors of Birchwood, of all the deaths and indignations, I discovered that loneliness is the worst.

* * *

I had to tell others eventually. I had to explain why she
wouldn't need a bunk space anymore. Why she wasn't
showing up for work.

"Lucky for her she'll have died quickly," Girder said.
"Unlike the rest of us, still slogging away. Don't you go
giving up," she added quickly. "Maybe one more winter,
that's all we'll have to last."

Easy for her to say. She'd outlast another ice age, she
was so tough.

In the Washery the only response I got to my news was
a nervous laugh from Hyena.

My fingers curled into a punch.

Don't hit her, said Rose.

Not even a little bit?

You know violence isn't the answer.

I sighed. Hyena kept her nose unbroken.

For a while I just worked. What else was there to do?
Bear sent me back to the drying ground. I didn't care.
Every frosty morning I took the laundry out. The washing
lines would be hung with iced dew. They looked like a
crisscross of giant spider webs. Every evening I brought the
laundry in. I beat the stiffness out of it and passed it to the
ironing room.

Rose tried tickling me sometimes, but I didn't feel a thing.

Was I even still alive? Once I could have sworn her lips brushed my cheek, but it was just a sock dangling from a peg.

Several times I saw Carla passing the lines of frosted washing. Pippa whined, and Carla jerked the leash. She saw me. I know she saw me, but she said nothing. Did nothing.

At night I lay on my bunk, eyes open. No tears. No sadness. No anger. I was numb.

Then one morning it snowed. There was ice on the inside of all the windows and white everywhere outside. The only bit of color to be seen was in my little length of red ribbon. I stroked the silk and knew what needed to be done. My shoulders were squared as I left the Washery with a wheeled laundry basket.

"Watch her," said Hyena with a giggle. "She's got that look."

"You think she's going to run for the fence?" squeaked Shrew.

"She's going to do something; that's for sure."

The fence was electrified. Deadly. Despairing Stripeys often chose to embrace the fence as a warm, shocking way to finish their lives.

I did not mess up the virgin snow near the fence with my shoe prints.

"I need fabric," I announced to the barrack that evening. "At least two meters of it. I'm going to make a dress."

"You've already got a dress," said Girder.

"Not a prison dress. I'm making a Liberation Dress."

It was impossible. Where could I get a handkerchief-size scrap of fabric, let alone enough for a dress? Add to that rare and precious items such as needle, thread, pins, fastenings, scissors. It would take a fairy-tale hero *years* of questing to gather such treasures.

I had until Birchwood was emptied.

Now that there were echoes of guns on the horizon, Birchwood was to be disbanded. Not today, not tomorrow, but soon. The signs were everywhere. Harassed guards. Chimneys smoking day and night. More bales and bundles than ever before leaving the Department Store by train.

There were cargoes of prisoners being transported out of Birchwood too. Rumor had it They were going to other camps, farther away from liberating armies. After so many years of boasting They could kill whoever they wanted, now there was a panic. It seemed They were desperate to hide evidence that places such as Birchwood had ever existed. It made me think of a school friend, back in the real world, who'd lost a board game and swept all the pieces to the floor, saying, "There, nobody knows who lost now!"

When I left Birchwood — however that happened — I'd go dressed like a real human being, in proper clothes. Not a bought dress, not a stolen dress, a dress I'd sewn myself, every single stitch *mine*.

* * *

209

Fabric.

I still had the crummy clothes Henrik had organized for our escape attempt. It had been risky keeping them hidden under my striped dress. Guards were brutal to anyone who showed initiative—like layering up to survive the cold. So I traded the thin jumper for half a pack of cigarettes. A *whole half packet* of cigarettes. The skirt and blouse weren't worth as much: more cigarettes and some bread. With these riches I could approach the Department Store.

Girder knew a girl who knew a girl who knew someone working in the Department Store. Taking her cut from my precious store of cigarettes, Girder made arrangements for the material I needed to be smuggled out to me. It was hugely risky, both for the girl who took the fabric and those who passed it along. I felt badly for getting other people involved. *They* didn't—payment was payment after all.

It took several tense days of waiting before a packet came my way. Girder let me open it in her private cubicle in one corner of the barrack block.

It was the ugliest fabric ever woven.

Girder burst out laughing. "Someone's puked all over it!" she cried. "Look, those orange squares could be bits of carrot!"

I felt like being sick myself. Perhaps on a mature woman, in a dim light, the crazy multicolored pattern would work. Not on a skinny young beanpole like me.

"It doesn't matter," I said valiantly. "It's good-quality fabric, there's enough of it, and it'll hang well."

"Can't wait to see it on!" Girder chuckled.

Scissors. There were two pairs that I knew of in use in the Laundry Mending Room. They never left the room. They were never unsupervised. Help came unexpectedly. Bear was ill. Hyena took temporary charge as boss of the Washery. I told her I was going to swap shifts with a seamstress from the Mending Room. Predictably, Hyena laughed.

"Ha, ha, nice try. Not a hope! Not a chance! Not going to happen!"

I didn't back down. "I need to borrow the mending-room scissors. To do that, I have to work in the Mending Room. You have to authorize it. If you don't, I'll find a way to steal those scissors, and I'll stab you in the heart with them while you're asleep."

Hyena opened her mouth to laugh . . . then thought better of it.

The Mending Room was *not* the Upper Tailoring Studio. By day there were about thirty women darning and repairing, watched over by a guard. By night there were thirty different women and no guard. I wrangled a visit during the late shift, when discipline was more relaxed. I'd heard the mending crew wasn't so bad. They swiped a lot of yarn and thread for themselves, or to barter, then smugly mended the guards' gray woolens in the wrong colors. Simple acts of defiance.

I found a spot to spread my fabric out.

"What are you doing?" said a heavyset slug of a woman, half-hidden behind a pile of holey socks. She must have been monumentally fat before Birchwood. Now she was swamped by folds of loose skin. Somehow this seemed even sadder than the skeleton-thin Stripeys I saw every day.

"I just need a bit of floor space," I told her briskly. "If you could move your feet, please."

Slowly the Slug retracted her wooden shoes. I spread my fabric across the floorboards and picked up the mending-room scissors.

"What are you making?" asked the Slug.

"A dress."

"Huh."

"Aren't you going to use a pattern?" squeaked a mouse-like woman, who was curled over a table, mending a torn shirt.

"Haven't got paper," I said, eyeing the fabric and wondering how best to get a dress out of it. I opened the scissors.

"What sort of dress?" squeaked the Mouse.

"A Liberation Dress. For me to wear when I get out of here, all right?"

"You're going to wear it? For real?"

Both Mouse and Slug stared at me.

I set the scissors down. "I suppose you're going to report me?"

Mouse looked at Slug. Slug looked at Mouse.

"Here, you'll need a tape measure," said Mouse timidly. She passed one over.

"Be quick," said Slug, who looked as if she'd never done anything speedy in her life. "I can see to your quota of sock darning while you're at it."

I blinked. "OK. That's good. Thank you." There were nice surprises left in the world after all. I picked the scissors up again.

Pins were no trouble — there were several on the mending-room floor, as I found out when I jabbed my hands and knees on them. Marta would've had a fit. In my head I heard her calling, *Pins!* Thread was easy too. I just teased out lengths from the cut edge of the material. Now all I needed was a needle. Slug nudged Mouse with one wooden shoe. Mouse twitched.

"Give her a needle," Slug said.

Mouse passed me one, all the while gaping at me as if I was starting a major revolution and she wanted to do her bit.

"Are you *really* going to sew your own dress?" she asked.

I nodded.

"Guards'll shoot you if they get wind of it," Slug announced.

I nodded again. "I know."

The pins, thread, and needle went into my secret pocket-bag. As for the cut dress pieces, I put them flat under my bunk mattress, hoping my scrawny weight would more or less iron them out. I meant to sew a little bit of the dress each day before lights-out.

Grandma had a cutting from a magazine pinned above her sewing table back home. It was advice on how to look nice while sewing. When she first read it she nearly killed herself laughing. I thought of the advice as I began work on my Liberation Dress:

When you sew, make yourself as attractive as possible. Put on a clean dress.

Clean dress? Fat chance. I sponged my striped sack of a dress down as often as I could at the Washery. As for being *attractive*, that was a complete nonstarter in Birchwood.

Being shaven also ruled out the next advice: *Have your hair in order, powder and lipstick applied.* If by *powder* they meant flaky skin from vitamin deficiency, I could manage that. *Lipstick* . . . lipstick cost a couple of *packs* of cigarettes in Birchwood. I'd heard of one tube of lipstick that did the rounds of a block, with every single woman dabbing some on her lips. They must've looked hideous, like painted skeletons. In their minds, having lipstick meant they were being normal women again.

Which was why I needed a Dress.

The final comment from the magazine explained the pre-sewing primping: apparently we'd all get twitchy worrying about someone dropping in, *or your husband might come home*, when we weren't looking our best. It wasn't husbands that worried me, of course, but more sinister visitors.

"Will you ask someone to keep lookout for guards?" I begged Girder the first evening I started sewing.

Girder sniffed. "Shouldn't you be worried about *me*, since *I'm* the law round here?"

I froze, suddenly more timid mouse than cunning fox.

"Just kidding, ha, ha!" Girder slapped me on the back, making my bones rattle. "The look on your face then . . . *hilarious*. But listen, little sewing girl, it's not just those feckwit guards you've got to watch for. Sneaky types in here could spread the word about what you're up to, for spite or ciggies. Just so you know, if you get caught I won't do anything to protect you." She mimed a gallow's noose.

It was pretty nerve-racking, taking up a needle for the first time since Carla had smashed my hand, and not just because of the fear of discovery. What if I couldn't do it? I stretched and wiggled my fingers lots first. I even got close to abandoning the whole project. A long-forgotten Grandma saying came to my rescue: *One stitch started is one nearer finished.* Her advice was much better than all that magazine twaddle.

I was shaking as I threaded the needle. My fingers ached. I took up one side seam. Pushed the needle in. Pulled it through. One stitch was followed by a second, a third, then countless more. The rhythm returned. It was almost like being happy.

I was tucked away on the top bunk, and I had my shoulders hunched for secrecy. Even so, other Stripeys climbed up to have a look. They hung around me like hungry monkeys.

215

As the dress began to take shape, more and more Stripeys wanted to watch. It was warmer having them there, if unnerving. I guess they were drawn by the simple normality of the scene — a girl sitting sewing.

I knew I'd have to do something to stop them from getting restless (and to distract them from the temptation to touch). So I took a deep breath and, in true Rose style, began. . . .

"Did I ever tell you about the time a poor dressmaker sewed herself a magic dress that could take her away to a City of Light?"

It wasn't even a good story. Rose would have been far better at it.

Everything was better when Rose was alive.

Many evenings later, Girder shouted up to my bunk, "You done yet?"

"Not yet."

The next evening: "Done yet?"

"Almost."

And finally: "How long's that feckin dress going to take?"

I answered, "It's ready. Don't expect anything fancy, though. It's not exactly couture."

"Not in that fabric," Girder snorted. "Come on then — give us a parade!"

I shook off a few bits of mattress straw, removed my striped sack, popped the dress over my head, and slowly eased my bones down from the top bunk. Clunky in my stupid shoes, I modeled it along the strip of floor space between the bunks and did a nice sashay around the stove in the center of the hut. Stripeys cheered feebly. Girder whistled. Then she shouted, "All right, *lights-out!*"

I took the dress off and spread it under my mattress, both to flatten out the creases and to keep it hidden. Success!

The next evening I came back from roll call and the Liberation Dress was gone. Stolen.

Girder offered to throttle the thief with their own intestines. No one confessed to the crime. Without the Dress, I felt as if there'd be no Liberation either. No Liberation, no homecoming, no Grandma, no Grandad, no hope.

"You could make another," Girder said.

I shook my head. "No point. I'm broke. No cigarettes, no spare bread, nothing left to barter with." It was a stupid idea anyway. Birchwood was Birchwood, and nothing would change that.

Cheer up, whispered an echo of Rose that night. *It's always darkest before the dawn.*

It *was* dark at four thirty the next morning, same as every dreary start to every dreary day. Some of the big camp lamps were out—a power cut?—so we crashed into each other as we ran to roll call. The air was freezing—like breathing cut glass.

Grandma had a special cupboard in the kitchen for her

cut-glass collection. There were wineglasses, sherry glasses, a trifle bowl, and even a bonbon dish etched with white doves. *Only for special occasions*, I was told. If I ever got home, and if those glasses and dishes still existed, I was going to get them all out and set the table for a feast. Wouldn't matter if there was only water in the wineglasses and bread in the bonbon dish. It would be a special occasion—we'd be alive and together.

Mind you, I wouldn't complain at all if there was a *proper* feast. Grandma's signature piece was a celebration cake smothered in white icing and dusted with sugar, just like the sugar being sprinkled on us at roll call. I opened my mouth to taste some. It was cold but not sweet: just snow.

When the whistle blew and I tried to move, I almost couldn't. My shoes had frozen to the ground. I scraped at the ice and frost until my fingers were raw and my shoes finally budged. By then my feet were too cold to feel the cold. Would it be so very bad if I just stayed still on that spot, like an ice sculpture?

Rub your feet, Rose-in-my-head said. *Don't get frostbite.*

Probably too late, I told her.

Did she sigh? I imagined she did. *You don't know how the story goes, Ella. There's always the next chapter.*

Yeah, yeah, and it's darkest before the dawn, and . . .

"Ella?"

Someone real was talking to me.

"What?"

"Are you Ella? Ella who sews?"

218

"Y—"

"This is for you." A packet was thrust into my arms. The messenger vanished.

No chance to open it. Not even to peek. Why did the Washery have to be so busy on this day of all days? There was *tons* of laundry to get through. Why were the guards still bothering about ironed shirts and clean socks? They knew the end was coming. They knew the guns were near. We knew They were making Lists: people who'd be leaving Birchwood, and those who'd have to stay.

Rumors spread faster than disease.

It's best to get out, some said. *They're going to burn the whole place to the ground then rake the ashes into fields as fertilizer.*

Best to stay here and hide, said others. *Wait for the liberators.*

They'll shoot us all first.

They'll shoot us all either way.

Finally, when the last sheet was folded and the last socks paired up, I got to see what was inside my mystery parcel.

Item — two meters of rich pink wool fabric

Item — one pair of fabric shears, gleaming silver

Items — one tape measure, one needle, and one spool of pink cotton thread

Item — a small paper package that rattled, labeled with a speech bubble that read *PINS!!*

Item (the one that finally made me cry) — five tiny round buttons covered with scraps of the pink material. Each button had been embroidered with a letter.

E R F S B

The embroidery was done in tiny chain stitches, nearly as neatly as Rose's handwork. At first I thought the letters would make a word. Then I realized they were initials: An *R* for Rosalind and an *E* for Ella. *F* for Francine. *S* for Shona. *B* for Brigid the hedgehog, who never smiled because of her teeth. There was no *M* for Marta.

As I cupped those teeny buttons in my palm, I felt a savage satisfaction: murderous though it was, Birchwood couldn't completely kill off love and generosity.

Told you so, whispered Rose in my ear.

Word of my Liberation Dress had spread, even as far as the workshop. And word that it had been stolen.

I hugged the new treasures close and I hoped there'd be time to make a second dress before the end came. Birchwood was restless — more chaotic, and therefore more dangerous. Change was coming.

"It's very *pink*," commented Girder, when she saw the new material. "I don't do pink. It's for frilly dolly-girls."

I shook out my work in progress. "My grandma always says, *Pink for perking up*. It's a happy color. When she's having a bad day, she swears putting on pink panties helps her feel cheerful."

"Pink panties? S'more my thing."

I bent low over my sewing to hide a smirk. Girder wouldn't have been so enthusiastic if she'd seen Grandma's giant pink balloon pants hanging out on the washing line.

Pink was a great antidote to War. You never saw dictators spouting hate on a pink podium. No pink flags flew above conquered towns. There were no Secret Police or invading armies or sadistic guards in pink. About the only people who wore pink uniforms were hairdressers and beauticians. It was hard to imagine them plotting world domination or genocide.

The morning after I was done making this second, miraculous Liberation Dress, I passed Girder during the early rush for roll call.

"Show me. Tonight!" she ordered.

At the Washery I cleaned myself as best I could, even my short hair. Standing at evening roll call I imagined putting on a dab of makeup and a spritz of perfume — something apple-fresh and light, *not* Blue Evening. I stepped into invisible high heels and fastened a necklace of invisible pearls.

Then I imagined scrubbing my face clean and ditching all the finery. This dress was about me being *me*, not about pretending to be some film star or fashion model.

The bunks were crammed full; they always were. What was shocking was the sheer number of women peering out at me when I arrived in the block. And the women from other barracks, hunkered down on the floor in front of the

221

bunks, clustered around the door and pressed up against any patch of wall.

"Is that her?" someone sniffed as I came in. "I thought you said it was a fashion show — proper posh like in the films."

I turned to hide outside.

Girder blocked my way. "We want to see the frock. Now."

There was nowhere private to change. I just had to undress right there in the middle of the block. Oddly, it wasn't so bad. Not like that awful first day in Birchwood when we went straight from civilized people to shivering nudity. Now, naked, I just felt completely, obviously *human*. A body, with a mind and a heart.

This body had a dress to wear, however.

"Ooh, that's a beauty!" I heard as I slipped my arms inside, then let it fall over my bones and bumps.

Others joined in. *Nice fit. . . . Not too tight. . . . Look at that skirt swish. . . . Smart matching belt. . . . and so PINK. . . .*

There weren't any mirrors so I couldn't see what I *really* looked like. But I know how I felt: *fabulous.* As I walked the length of the block, careful not to tread on anyone, I imagined stepping out in the City of Light, with blossoms falling all around me. I got to the end of the block and turned back. Stopped.

Silence.

That was a bit off-putting. Didn't they realize the work it had taken to make this dress? Couldn't they understand how special it was, with the five embroidered buttons going down the front, over my heart?

Then I saw the faces near me. They were wet with tears.

More slowly this time, I began walking back. Thin arms reached out, and thin hands pulled at the frock, just to touch the pink.

I heard someone murmur, *Do you remember colors like that?*

As I got to the end of my catwalk, there was a sudden eruption of noise as everyone spoke, and laughed and cried, and remembered dresses from days long past. It got so rowdy we almost didn't hear the commotion at the barrack door.

"Guards! Quick! Quiet!" came the warning.

I was trapped. My fingers fumbled at the belt buckle and the buttons, desperately trying to get the dress off before it was spotted. Stripeys jostled around me, hiding me from predators in the center of the pack.

It was no killer lion, however. No guard with a whip and a stick. Three faces I recognized came into view. Three friends fought to get closer.

"Are you there, Ella? Are we too late?"

"Francine? Shona? Is that you?"

"Large as life, sweetheart, and just as ugly!" laughed Francine.

Shona smiled and waved. She looked too weak to stand properly. I saw that Francine was propping her up.

Francine pushed the third girl nearer. "And do you remember —"

"*B* for Brigid!" I interrupted, touching the *B* button on my dress. "Of course I do."

Brigid the hedgehog flashed a shy smile, then quickly put her hand to her mouth to hide it.

I should've said *thank you* in a million eloquent ways. I should've curtsied and bowed and told them endlessly how kind they'd been to organize everything for my dress. But, overwhelmed by their kindness, I couldn't say anything. I just cried.

"We heard about your last dress being stolen," Francine explained. "We had to try to help. Thank god Marta never noticed what we were up to."

Shona took a deep breath. Even speaking was hard work for her now. How could she be so thin, so ill, and still keep such a bright light in her eyes?

"You made a dress for *you*, not for Them!" she said in a faint voice.

Francine nodded. "About time They didn't have everything Their own way."

"Damn right," said Girder.

"It's a really good dress," Francine said, all matter of fact. "Pink's cheerful, isn't it? Anyway, this morning a little bird sent word that you were done."

"Not so little," said Girder, flexing her arms in a body-builder pose.

"Fair enough. A chunky big bird sent word you'd be trying it on, and we just had to come see. What d'you call it — a Liberation Dress?"

Mute, I nodded.

Liberation. The word spread like fire through the block.

"Do you really think we're getting out of here?" Shona asked.

"Let's feckin hope so!" shouted Girder.

"Out! Out! Everybody out!"

A guard threw open the Washery door and screamed at the girls inside. When they just stood there in shock, soapy water dripping from their hands, she began hitting them with her whip handle. Then they moved.

I was watching from the drying ground, hidden behind lines of underwear. It was time.

If they were emptying the Washery, it meant the guards were going too. They wouldn't want to stay at work without clean socks, poor babies.

"All of you rats to roll call!" screamed the guard. "Right now! Run!"

I dodged between the laundry lines and managed to catch the eye of one of the girls near the back of the group. My bad luck — it was Shrew. I signaled to her: *Over here.*

She skittered between undershirts and pants, closely followed by Hyena and a couple of others.

"We have to go to roll call," Shrew squeaked. "Or do you think we should hide?"

"It's up to you what you do; I don't care," I said. "Whatever you decide, you'll need to have food and warmer clothes than these rags."

"Where from?" scoffed Shrew. "Have you got a magic wand?"

Casually I fingered the gray-white wool hanging on the line.

I can't say it was a treat to feel long johns worn by Them against my skin. Better than freezing, at least. I took socks too. The other girls silently watched me layer up in warm clothes, then there was a scramble to copy.

I wasn't going to stop there. I had my pink dress on already — I hadn't dared leave that unguarded in the barrack. Now I had plans to get more layers.

"Who wants to go shopping?" I asked.

Shrew scowled. "Haven't you seen the guards in trucks roaming around? They're shooting prisoners for fun."

I knew that. They were like big-game hunters herding prey.

"Suit yourselves," I said. "I'm off to the Department Store, with or without you. They stole all our stuff when we got here. Why shouldn't we get something back?"

For months — *years* — trains had been rattling out of Birchwood carrying goods from the Department Store. As order collapsed, valuables were *still* being looted. We narrowly missed being mown down by two trucks piled high with locked boxes. Money, probably, and gold. I thought of the "diamond" ring Carla had given me and wondered whose finger it would end up on. Not mine, for sure.

I'd trade diamonds for decent boots any day.

There were still people in the Little Store. I thought I heard glass smashing. There was a stink of something strong in the air . . . possibly Blue Evening perfume.

The Big Store looked as if a team of angry ogres had played rugby inside. Clothes and shoes were tossed everywhere. I scrambled into a hut and began to pull at piles of clothes. Other scavengers fought me for my finds. I fought back. First, a wool coat and sweater. The coat was quite fashionable, with big padded shoulders. It didn't match the ski hat and scarf I got next. Who cared? Getting an actual pair of gloves was lucky, though I'd've settled for odd ones. Decent footwear was the hardest. It felt wrong, somehow, stepping into someone else's shoes, but I grabbed a pair of fleece-lined boots and an extra pair of socks to pad them out.

It was the craziest shopping expedition I'd ever been on, like a parody of New Year sales.

"Hurry, hurry," I called to the other Washery girls. "I smell smoke!"

We assembled at the hut door. Hyena pointed and laughed at how bulky we all were, like multicolored snowmen. It was stupid, but all of us joined in laughing too. My outfit didn't seem so funny when I suddenly wanted to pee and realized that I now had a million layers on.

* * *

Not long after, flames took hold of the Department Store. If They couldn't profit from all the loot, They were going to make sure no one else could.

"Hey—you're not leaving, are you?" A fist thumped my arm. I whirled around. There was Girder, with not one but two girlfriends hanging off her.

I froze. Girder could be friendly when she wanted, but she was a boss after all, and I was loaded up with stolen goods. "We . . . we . . . organized some clothes."

"No kidding. I'm heading to do the same before the whole store burns. We're sticking here in Birchwood. Guards are running like rabbits. If we can avoid getting shot or blown up, it's just a matter of time before we're liberated. As for them"—she jerked her head in the direction of roll call, where Stripeys were assembling—"they're all going to be herded as far away from liberation as possible. It's nothing but a death march in the snow: no one's meant to live to tell tales. Come back to the barrack and hide with us. Be here when we walk out of those gates as free people."

It was tempting. I believed what she said about Them not wanting us to survive. Also, part of me didn't want to say good-bye to Rose's ghost by leaving.

I shook my head. "I'm going. I've just got to get home. Find my grandma . . ."

"Yeah, yeah, you in your Liberation Dress! Good luck to ya, sewing girl. I'll be there at your dress shop, first customer. Got to keep my ladybirds looking nice, haven't I, darlings?"

228

She chucked one of her girlfriends on the cheek, then dragged them away. I ran to roll call.

It was a sign of how harassed the guards were that we didn't get shot on the spot for wearing nonprison clothes. I sensed rather than saw other Stripeys shiver and fall—mostly women just in a thin dress without stockings or coat. Sometimes they could be helped to their feet. Mostly they never moved again. I couldn't bear to watch. I went cross-eyed trying to look at the snowflakes that landed on my nose. Around me there were dogs snarling. Motorbikes growling. Guards shouting.

We ran in lines of five and groups of five hundred. Down Birchwood's main street we stumbled. I had Shrew on one side and Hyena on the other. Other Washery girls made up the row of five behind me. Soon we reached the main gate, with its arch of metal that declared: WORK SETS YOU FREE.

Once I left there'd be nothing to tie me to Rose. Nothing except the red ribbon tucked into my glove, nestling in the curve of my palm.

Just outside the gate a man in an immaculate uniform was watching us leave. I nearly tripped and fell at the sight of him. It was the man I'd seen in the photograph at Madam's house, back in the summer. Madam's husband—the commandant himself!

Did he see people passing or just stripes?

We ran on.

* * *

We ran on. Gray ghosts in a white dreamscape. We ran through a strange land, with hedges and houses — real houses. Windows were shuttered. Curtains were drawn.

We ran on. Those who couldn't keep running crumpled at the side of the road, or fell under the feet of whoever followed. Shrew kept keening, "I can't do this, I just can't do this." I had my own silent chant: *I can do this, I will do this.*

We ran on. The sun rose. The sky barely brightened. Still it snowed. The cold bit through all my layers of clothing. Only the red ribbon in my hand kept me truly warm.

We ran on. Hyena gave a little hoarse giggle — "Beddy-byes time . . ." Then she fell forward and pulled me over too. I scrambled up before a guard's whip could find us.

"Come on, get up, keep going," I said.

"Just for a minute," Hyena gasped. Her face was white as solid ice.

"You can't stop. We all have to keep moving." I practically dragged her along with me, one arm hooked under hers.

"Don't be such a bully," Shrew said. "You always think you know best. *I'm* going to have a rest too. I'm on my last legs. Can't you even see that?"

"They'll have to last a lot longer yet," I snapped. "Give me a hand here, why don't you?"

Two other Washery girls caught up with me. Without a word they scooped up Hyena and trotted along with her. And we ran on.

230

Those without shoes suffered most. People who think clothes are frivolous haven't ever been barefoot in snow for mile after mile after mile. When I had my dress shop I'd design warm things as well as glamorous ones. Lots and lots of winter woolies.

That was how I kept myself going—telling myself every step I took brought me nearer to the dress shop.

Every so often we had to run on the banks or ditches at the side of the road, when big cars with headlamps came past. One car didn't wait for us to pass. In the back seat I saw an officer in a smart hat, several children, and Madam H., owner of my beautiful sunflower dress with Rose's embroidery.

Behind Madam's car came trucks full of boxes and suitcases. The convoy sprayed us all with chilly slush. In the confusion, I lost sight of the Washery lot. Shrew, Hyena—they could have been anywhere in the rows of hunched shoulders and snow-whitened heads.

I ran on.

When it was truly too dark to run anymore, They herded us into fields and told us to sleep. On the frozen earth. Same again after a second day of running, running, running, stumbling, running. No one had a face anymore, just frozen breath and eyes on the back of the runner in front. Everything was a blur. When someone stopped or fell, if she didn't get up quickly enough, the guards would shoot. If someone tried to break free of the stampede to run across the fields or into a building as we passed, the guards would shoot.

In some villages people threw bread onto the road as we passed. In others they sprinkled shards of broken glass.

Every step is one step closer to the dress shop. That was my mantra.

I had the red ribbon coiled close in my hand. I could survive this. I could make it. I would make it. No point crying — tears just froze. I ran on ran on ran on and thought of what my dress shop would look. Mile after mile, I planned the décor, furnished the fitting rooms and showrooms and offices and workshops. I bought fabric and trimmings. Hired bead-sewers and feather-workers, embroiderers and finishers. I welcomed clients, sketched designs, draped mannequins, and made a fortune.

After many miles I became too tired even to dream.

On the second night some Stripeys just lay down and let the snow cover them — human drifts. My group stopped near a half-ruined cowshed. I made straight for it and jostled past the other canny souls who'd had the same idea. There was ice on the bare floor and not much else. With enough of us bundled together we might make it through the night.

I took a glove off long enough to reach into my layers and retrieve a hunk of bread. One second later the glove was gone. I lashed out —"Mine! Give it to me!" The thief fought back, a vicious biting bitch. A shark.

"Marta!"

The thief recoiled, breathing hard. She still had my glove. "You? *Ella?* You're still alive?"

"No thanks to you."

Marta's bitter laugh turned into a hacking cough. "Told you you're a survivor. Like me."

"Where are the others?"

"How should I know? They were slowing me down."

That made me bristle. "They were good friends. They sent me a present — fabric and things to make me a dress."

"Ha, yes, the famous Liberation Dress," said Marta. "They thought they were so cunning, organizing it behind my back. I knew about it, of course. How's liberation working for you now?"

"Give me my glove," I fumed.

"Give me some bread!"

"You laughed at Rose when she shared her bread. Now you're asking *me* to share *mine?*"

Marta seemed to slump. Suddenly she wasn't a shark. Not even a seamstress who'd trained in all the very best places and shouted *Pins!* all day long.

"Never mind about that," she said. "I'm starving. You've got bread. What would your precious Rose do?"

What would Rose do?

Rose would've told a story about desert islands with white sands, or steam baths and bubbling hot pools. Using nothing but words, she'd conjure up warm blankets and hot drinks.

Rose, I miss you so much.

* * *

Marta wolfed down the piece of bread I gave her. She hadn't given me my glove back. I sat with my one bare hand tucked inside my coat.

"Can't you share a layer?" Marta whined. "You've got so many, and I've just got what I grabbed from the workshop."

She was wearing a dainty crochet cardigan over her dress, and over that a coat with no sleeves — an unfinished project. Still feeling the bruises of how I'd fought for my warm clothes, I wasn't exactly keen on parting with them. As the night went on Marta's coughing got harsher, as if her very lungs were being shredded. In the end I unwound my scarf and thrust it at her.

By faint moonlight I saw how wrecked she looked. The tip of her nose was blue-black, as were her cheeks. Frostbite. She had shoes, but they were just light leather town brogues, tied on with a piece of string. No socks. Her legs were cold as marble and blotched like her face.

She turned away, ashamed.

Morning.

Get up! Get out! Get moving! screamed the guards outside our cowshed. Some of the human snowdrifts moved. Some would never move again.

Marta didn't stand a chance on her own. We both knew that.

What would Marta do?
Save herself and nobody else.
What would Rosalind do?
Nothing. Rose was dead.
What would Ella do?

"Come on," I said gruffly. "We'd better get moving."

"I hope no one sees me in this awful getup," Marta moaned. She had my hat jammed over her headscarf, my sweater over her cardigan, and one of my gloves to keep swapping between two hands.

We ran.

By then it was less of a run and more of a shamble. Everyone's eyes were glazed. Everyone's feet dragged. Even the guards looked miserable. Snow clumped on our shoes and boots, making movement even tougher. That dress shop seemed farther away than ever before, lost in a haze of hunger and exhaustion. Gunshots were more frequent. Surely the guards would run out of bullets soon?

The road was uneven. Stripeys tripped and tumbled over. Marta tripped. Something snapped. Her face bleached and she fell, dragging me with her.

"S'broken," she sobbed. "My leg."

"Not your leg. Maybe a tendon," I said, hoisting her up. "Come on, we can't stop."

235

"I can't *move!*" she screamed.

"You can't stay here—they'll *shoot* you!" I screamed back. A guard was coming closer.

"You *can* move and you *will*," I hissed through clenched teeth. I got hold of her under the arms.

I ran while Marta hopped and cried and cursed me. She was as heavy as a sack of concrete, and far more difficult to handle. To keep going, I told her about the dress shop, the cake shop, the bookshop, and the City of Light. It wasn't such a beautiful dream now that Rose wouldn't be making the dresses, eating the cakes, or reading the books to me. Now Rose was just a memory. Through days of running through white snow and white sky, it seemed as if the whole world had vanished, leaving only memories. I ran in a trance, lost in a lifetime of memory fragments, like pieces of a patchwork quilt . . . Grandad teaching me to ride a bike. Falling off the bike. Grandma making me wash the dishes. Grandma letting me lick cake batter from the bowl. First day of school. Last day of school . . .

Streams of Stripeys stumbled past us in the snow. We were going too slowly. . . . We were grinding to a halt.

"Marta, *please* . . . keep moving. You know what will happen if you don't."

There was a guard not far behind.

"You go," Marta wheezed. "Go on—leave me."

"You've no idea how much I want to!" I said, along with a few swear words borrowed from Girder. "Doesn't mean I'm going to."

I managed to drag her a few more paces, then I heard Marta gasp. Her eyes widened. She'd noticed the guard. She gave a cry and twisted her body, pushing me ahead. When the bullet came it hit her, not me.

It hit her, not me, shoving her down, with me pinned underneath. I bit snow. Somehow I managed to turn, to find Marta was lying on her back on top of me.

Her blood was awfully red and warm as it spread across her dress.

A second, deafening shot.

Marta's body jerked, then was still. Her eyes stayed open, showing only the whites.

Boots crunched slowly closer. I pushed and pushed at Marta's body but could barely shift it.

"Thought it was you," said a cold voice from high up. "What are the odds?"

I saw nothing but the boots at first. They were thick hiking boots lined with fur. Squinting higher, I saw dark trousers, a black cloak, and two small black button eyes.

"Carla!"

"Well . . . isn't this fun?"

With a grunt, Carla squatted at my side. Her breath was a cloud. She smelled of sweat and Blue Evening.

"What's that you're holding on to there? Huh. Still clutching that stupid scrap after all this time?"

Carla gave the red ribbon a tug. I held on tightly. For a

moment it was almost as if we were holding hands, right there in the snow. She tugged some more. I gripped that ribbon like it was life itself.

"Mine," I said.

Carla licked cold-cracked lips and straightened up. "Not wearing my ring? I *knew* you'd sell it. Ungrateful little rat. Your Sort, you don't know what friendship is."

There she stood, gazing down at me, with something like pity in her eyes. Snow settled on her black cloak.

"Don't you know there's no point running anymore? It's over — all over. The War's lost. Pippa's lost too. Run down by a truck yesterday. Had to shoot her. Put her out of her misery — poor thing. How are *you* still alive?"

My lungs were squashed but I managed one word. "Hope."

Carla snorted. "There is no hope. You're going to starve or freeze to death, whichever comes first. Shooting you will be a kindness."

She stepped back. Her leather boots creaked. She raised her black gun and fired. My body jolted.

Oh, how funny, I thought. *I wonder . . .*

It's OK, said Rose. *I'm waiting for you.*

Pink

I suppose there must have been blood, and lots of it, freezing red around my cold body. I don't remember any of that. I woke to find myself buried in a soft quilt sprigged with pink flowers. A square of blue hanging on the wall turned out to be a window. I heard a chink of china.

"Ready for some tea?" came a warm voice.

Being dead was strange. Warmer than I'd expected.

"Stay still, I'll bring it to you," said the voice.

That was good, because I was kitten-weak. A cup was put to my lips. I slurped tea. It was milky and shockingly sweet.

"Eh, looks like you needed that," said the voice. It belonged to a large, round woman in a pastel-pink apron. "You need feeding up too. Not a scrap of meat on your bones, like my old heifer that got sickly. Spoon-fed her, I did, night and day. Soon got her back on her feet, right as rain."

"You're . . . a farmer?"

"Hardly surprising, since this is a farm. Found you in the ditch, edge of my turnip field, I did. You and one other. She was long past helping, mind. Thought you were too, till my dog licked your hand and it twitched."

Somewhere in my cotton-ball brain, a memory glittered.

"My ribbon? Have you got my ribbon? I have to find it!"

I was pushing the quilt away, pushing the farmer away, doing my best to stand up, but the two thin sticks attached to my hips wouldn't move an inch.

"Eh, settle down," said the farmer, holding me still. "If you mean that mucky scrap of silk, I've kept it safe. Well-washed, mind, like all that hodgepodge of clothes you had on."

"I want it." I said, sinking back into strange comfort.

She tucked the quilt back in place. "You'll get it, don't fret. Now, let's start with simple things. What shall I be calling you?"

Out of habit I reeled off my Birchwood number. The farmer blinked.

"How about a *name?*" she asked gently. "I'm Flora. I know—daft name for a big lump like me. I was born in the spring, and Mother had a fancy for flowers. Lucky she didn't call me Blossom, I've always thought."

My name. She actually wanted my name.

"I'm . . . I'm Ella. I sew."

I didn't mean to go straight back to sleep. I had no idea it was possible to sleep so long and so deeply. At one point I woke to see the farmer's shoes inches from my face.

"What are you doing down there, lass?" she asked, bending to look at me, curled under the bed.

I was ashamed. The floor felt more natural. The bed was too soft after what I'd been used to.

"I . . . I didn't want to get your nice sheets dirty."

"Them's only old sheets, mended more times than I can remember. Reckon you could do with a proper bath, mind, not just the sponge wash I gave you first off, before I put the dressing on. Nasty wound that. Bullet must've gone through and through. You were lucky."

With a jolt I remembered a gunshot. The skewer of pain in my chest. I touched a wad of cotton bound around my ribs.

"It'll be bruised still, and it'll scar," said Flora. "No dancing jigs and splitting it open again."

Jigs? Oh. She was joking.

"Why . . . ?" I started to ask, before tears overtook me. "Why are you helping me? Didn't you see my prison stripes? The star sewn onto my dress? Didn't you see what I am?"

"Eh, lass, don't think on that. I saw a girl, that's all. Just a girl. Now get back in this bed and eat the stew I've brought. It should be light enough to go down nicely and stay down, for all your stomach must be shrunk to the size of a pea. Quick now — I've cattle to feed."

She asked me once about Birchwood.

"We heard something about a place . . . prisoners . . . chimneys . . . but I just couldn't believe it was real," she said in a hushed voice.

"Neither could I . . . but it was," I whispered back.

* * *

243

She was a queen to me, this poor farmer. A queen in a patched apron and a creaky house. When I jolted awake at four thirty each morning, expecting whistles, shouts, and roll call, Flora was already trudging through snow to her barn, coaxing breakfast from her one surviving milk cow. Then she'd be feeding up the beef cattle and getting on with a hundred other jobs. Mostly I slept, curled to the edge of the soft mattress so as to make room for the girl who wasn't there. When awake, I counted the rosebuds speckling the wallpaper and watched clouds scud past the window. There were photos on the shelf above the fire.

"My daughter," Flora said, following my gaze to a portrait of a pretty young woman. "She's off looking after injured soldiers. I'm hoping she makes a better nurse than milkmaid. I was always catching her with her nose in a book, when she was meant to be doing chores. My dear departed husband was just the same—read, read, read. Here, do you like stories?"

I shook my head. No story could be as magical or as sorrowful as surviving. *Oh, Rose, my storyteller.*

There was no answering whisper.

"Go on, have a book by the bed," said Flora. "To stop you brooding. Eh—don't think I can't hear you cry in your sleep, nightmares and all. Stands to reason. Daresay you've had it rough. Here, try this one. My lass loved it, as did my husband, may he rest in peace."

She passed me a little book with a cracked spine. It was a book I'd seen before, back in Birchwood's Department

Store, when Rose had gone up to that guard and said that her mama had written the book he was reading, and he threw it in the fire.

Silly Rose and her stories. Telling me she was a countess who lived in a palace, and her mother some great writer.

I opened the cover. I didn't recognize the title or the author's name. It was the dedication that made me sit bolt upright in bed, bullet wound or no bullet wound.

To my darling daughter, Rosalind.
I hope great things of her.

Always it came back to hope.

Alone in that bedroom I stroked my red ribbon. Behind me was Birchwood, a place so awful I already couldn't believe it existed. Ahead of me was the next chapter.

I decided I'd had enough of bed. Enough of spoon-feeding. Enough of nightmares. I eased out from under the quilt and found my clothes. They were washed, ironed, and folded onto a chair.

I could hardly bear to touch the striped Birchwood dress. Flora could rip it up into cleaning rags as far as I was concerned, and *burn* the star badge I'd worn for so long. I had warm long johns and socks at least, and of course the beautiful Liberation Dress. Apart from the bullet hole, which could be sealed with careful darning, it had survived that terrible run through the snow very well. That showed how good the fabric was. Grandma always said, *Buy the best quality you can afford. Cheap rubbish is no economy.*

Grandma would like the dress, I was sure of it. I slipped it on carefully and stroked each of the five embroidered buttons. I was free now. Free to . . . to go downstairs. First things first. I held on to the banister for support.

A grizzled gray-and-white cat looked up from the fireplace when I shuffled into the kitchen. Flora was at the kitchen sink, scrubbing wizened little potatoes. Her clothes were badly made and badly fitting, but I wouldn't have swapped her for all the fashion models in the City of Light.

"Hello?"

Flora jumped to hear my voice behind her. "Now then! Look at you, all dolled up. That's a fine dress you've got. I thought so when I washed it. Nicely made and everything. Proper shop-bought quality, that."

"Can I help?"

She paused. She wasn't used to anyone interfering. "You can be washing these potatoes. I'm doing a stew."

It was a simple job. I moved slowly so I wouldn't set the bullet wound bleeding.

While the stew cooked in the oven, I washed dishes and dried them. Flora put on her coat and scarf to go out in the yard.

"Can I help?" I asked again.

"Out there? One gust of wind and you'd blow away! I can't see *you* farming or chopping wood. What else can you do?"

My face broke into a wide grin. "Have you got a needle and thread?"

Winter thawed. An old man on a bicycle brought us news that although the War wasn't yet over, it had passed us by, and the end was near.

"Thank goodness for that," said Flora. "I wasn't pleased at the thought of tank tracks on my fields."

We didn't exactly celebrate the news. One of the cows was in calf and it began to birth just before teatime. I found myself on the end of a rope with Flora, hauling that new life into the world, hoofs first.

Flora wiped her hands on her trousers. "You're going soon, aren't you?" she said.

"I'll stay as long as you need me."

"Go," she said. "But remember — you're welcome here whenever, War or no War."

"I'm really, really grateful for everything. It's just, I've *got* to go . . . home."

"Of course you do, lass. Of course you do."

I knew from looking at the farm's worn atlas that I was hundreds of miles from home. Flora had shown me which speck on the map was the nearest village to the farm, then I traced a line all the way to my town. Even supposing all the territory had been liberated, how was I, penniless and alone, to travel so far?

One of Grandma's sayings danced in my mind: *Cross that bridge when you come to it, or swim the river if you have to.*

That evening I examined the coat I'd worn out of Birchwood. It needed remodeling. We didn't exactly gorge ourselves at the farm, but I was still putting weight on. One by one I cut the coat seams to let them out a bit. A thought struck me: during my first trip to the Department Store, that mole of a girl had said something about people hiding valuables in their clothes.

I found the money—a big wad of it—in the shoulder pads, stuffed between tufts of horsehair. I shivered to think of the fate of the nameless woman who'd stitched her savings away. Her foresight was my windfall.

I left a bundle of money under my pillow, so Flora would find it after I'd gone. I couldn't face her thanking me. Even if it had been an armful of gold and jewels, like a treasure trove from one of Rose's stories, it still couldn't repay her for the most priceless thing of all: human kindness.

I wrote a note. It just said, *To Flora. From Ella. You saved my life.*

On the day I left, Flora loaned me a hairbrush for the little waves of hair now covering my scalp. I slipped on my Liberation Dress, laced my boots, and buttoned up my coat. Flora was wearing one of the smart new shirts I'd made for her and a new pair of work trousers, also sewn by me. She handed over a packet of sandwiches and shortbread cookies.

"Got your red ribbon?"

I nodded. Couldn't speak.

"All sorted then. Good luck, Ella."

I just stood there, stiff and awkward. I turned to go. Thought, *What would Rose do?* I turned back and gave my new friend a long, warm, grateful hug. And left.

I said good-bye to the cat, the cows, the chickens, the farm dog, and Marta. Marta had been laid to rest under a grassy mound covered in daisies. A simple wooden grave marker had her name on it and the date she died.

I walked up the lane alone, with my head high. Time to go home.

First I walked to the nearest village. Then, because there was no other transportation, I walked from there to the nearest town. Here there were buses running, and a huge clamor of people — walking, talking, cycling, driving, shopping . . . just as if everything was normal. And it was, for them. For me it was like being a child again, seeing things for the first time. Look — a grocery shop. Over there — a baker's. In that window — a reflection. Me. A tall, serious girl in a tight coat and sensible boots. A flash of pink showed as I walked.

It was hard to believe that all of this had existed at the same time I was in the mud and dust and ash of Birchwood.

From this town I caught a bus to the next. Then a train. Another train. Another town. A tram. Eventually my boots took me down familiar streets to the house where I used to live.

My house. I practically ran to the door, ready to shout, *It's me! It's Ella! I'm home!*

The door was locked. I pressed the bell. No answer. The windows were blank. When I peered in I saw the familiar kitchen stools, the ones that made farty noises when you sat on them, and the china cupboard, now full of old newspapers, not Grandma's cut-glass collection.

A woman sweeping the yard next door eyed me suspiciously. "You can ring the doorbell as much as you like — there's nobody home."

"I'm looking for my grandparents."

"In that house? Two young doctors live there. Nobody old."

"Don't you remember me? I'm Ella. This was my home."

She squinted at me. "I don't know anything about that."

"But my grandparents — where are they? Were they taken to . . . to Birchwood?" I hated the taste of that word in my mouth.

The neighbor stepped back behind her broom. "You don't want to believe all those horror stories! Birchwood indeed!"

It was no better at the newsstand. This was the shop I'd popped into almost every day of my former life, to buy bits and bobs. Tobacco for Grandad, magazines for me and Grandma. The shelves weren't so full now, thanks to the War. The same twitchy hamster-woman stood at the till, though, with her jangly gold earrings.

"Hello, love, what can I get you?"

"It's me, Ella! I'm back!"

Hamster looked me up and down. For a moment it felt as if she was seeing a Stripey with a shaved head and stupid wooden shoes. I almost reeled off my camp number.

"Ella? You can't be! She was just a schoolgirl. You're *Ella*? Really? I'd never have known you! Aren't you all smart and grown-up now? You look well. Not had a bad War, then? Your Sort always fall on your feet, eh?"

That threw me. I resisted the urge to run away there and then. Girls in Liberation Dresses do not flee the enemy.

"I'm looking for my grandparents. Do you know where they are?"

Hamster waved her arms. Bracelets tinkled. "Oh, they left. Went somewhere else. Somewhere east maybe. I can't keep track of what my customers get up to. There's been a War on, you know. Come to think of it, they owed me some money. That's right, I've got it here in my account book. For tobacco and a magazine. It's good you've come by. You can square up, can't you?" She told me how much.

For a few seconds I couldn't breathe, let alone speak, I was so angry. Then, looking Hamster straight in the eyes the whole time, I reached for my precious hoard of money. I counted out, to the last exact coin, the amount my grandparents had owed and pushed the money across the counter. I held Hamster's gaze for a long, scornful moment, and turned to go.

When I left the shop she still hadn't picked up the money.

251

My Birchwood boots took me along the pavement to my old school, past the spot where I'd been snatched off the street a year ago.

I felt the ghost of a school satchel strap on my shoulder.

But I wasn't a schoolgirl anymore. I had to decide where to go and what to do next. I took another train.

The City of Light was full of flowers.

There was a florist's stall at the station when I arrived, with buckets of color. There were flowery weeds nodding their heads from odd cracks and corners of bullet-damaged buildings. And there were flowers on the dresses—glorious floral prints that declared to the world, *It's spring again!* Spring, and the city was liberated, and the War was almost over.

A fabulous metal tower stretched up above the city rooftops to the sky, way above even the highest buildings. It was decorated with flags. It reminded me of Henrik—all bold and glorious.

For all the flowers and fashions and flags, I couldn't leave Birchwood behind. It was there, gnawing at my stomach when I saw a generous housewife throw stale bread to the birds and I remembered being so hungry I'd've crawled on the ground to snatch it up too.

It was there when I caught sight of a sign in a shop window

advertising Blue Evening perfume. Then my nose clogged with the stink of Carla's scent.

It was there whenever I saw stripes.

People saw me in my pink Liberation Dress and smiled. I didn't smile back, not often. I couldn't stop looking at random strangers and wondering, *What would you have been like in Birchwood?* Oh, but it was nice to look lovely again! To feel properly washed and dressed.

I had traveled over a thousand miles just to arrive at this place, at this day in the year. It *was* today, I was certain. Hadn't Rose made me memorize the date?

Today was the day Rose and I had vowed to meet if we got separated, in a park, under the falling blossoms of an apple tree.

I'd asked directions from a porter at the train station. He'd scratched his head and rubbed his bristly chin. "A park with an apple tree? Opposite a cake shop and bookshop and a hairdresser's, you say?"

"And a dress shop. Opposite a dress shop too."

"I don't know about any dress shop, but I reckon I know the park and the bakery."

There was no one to give orders, to tell me when to sleep, when to wake, when to cringe, when to grovel. I ate when I pleased, as long as my money lasted, and I slept wherever I found myself at nightfall — in refugee hostels, on sofas of kind strangers, and even on station benches. Some people shunned me when they heard I'd no family, or when they guessed where I'd come from. Others — the real humans — shared what little they had.

"We didn't know," they said. "We never guessed."

On my travels from the farm, to home, to here, I'd crossed paths with other survivors. We knew each other at once. No words needed. No need to show our number. When we met, we kept company for a while. We shared the names of people we'd known at Birchwood, and people we wanted to find.

There was no news of my grandparents.

I reached the park. There was no fence, just metal stumps where the railings had been shorn off to be turned into bombs or tanks or whatever the War machine needed. A space without borders. Not a jag of barbed wire in sight. No watchtowers. No sentries.

On the other side of the street, there was a row of shops, just as Rose had described them. A cake shop (open), a hat shop, bookshop, and hairdresser's (closed), and an empty dress shop, with no sign and a headless display mannequin in the window.

All those times Rose had spun stories, and she'd been telling the truth. I was stupid, stupid, stupid to have never quite believed her. Easier to think I knew best and she was only daydreaming.

My boots walked me across the street, dodging cars and

vans and bikes. There was a cleaning lady on her knees just inside the open doorway of the dress shop, calmly polishing the floor with big yellow mitts on her hands. It reminded me of polishing the fitting-room floor at the Upper Tailoring Studio. For one silly moment I looked at the cleaner and thought, *Is it Rose?* The woman sensed me there and turned.

It wasn't Rose.

This was a woman in her fifties, perhaps, with a shock of white hair and lines creasing her face. She had an unlit cigarette tucked behind one ear, a battered paperback novel crammed in her apron pocket, and a sprig of pink blossoms pinned to her apron front. When she spoke, her voice was surprisingly soft and cultured.

"Can I help you?"

I shook my head, and turned back across the street to the park.

After a night of rain the park lawn was so green. The grass was sprinkled with buttercups. I thought of Rose and her daft idea that if you hold the flowers under someone's chin you can see if they like butter. I picked a buttercup. I couldn't see under my own chin. Not to worry. I knew I liked butter anyway.

There were daisies, too. Carla told me you should pluck the daisy petals off one by one and say, *She loves me, she loves me not . . .*

I left the daisies.

I wandered along neat pathways, past a fountain, to the

center of the park, where an apple tree spread blossomy branches, right where Rose said it would be. I wished I'd listened better when she was still alive.

The ribbon was more pink than red, after all the washings. I meant to tie it to a branch of the tree, just as Rose and I had planned to do, all those ages ago in Birchwood. Instead of a celebration of surviving together, it could be a small act of remembrance for a girl whose thousand acts of kindness made her more of a hero to me than any general.

I stroked the ribbon, suddenly shy of doing something so personal when there were other people around. Would they laugh, or, worse, ask questions?

There was an old man walking a dog — a fluffy sort of hearth-rug dog, with a ball in its mouth, not a prisoner's leg. There was a tall man with his arm around a short woman. They were laughing, and she put her face up to be kissed. There was an elegant young lady sitting on one of the park benches, with her knees and ankles neatly together, a little bag in her lap, and the most ridiculous pink hat pinned to her short curls. She was definitely watching me.

I turned my back to everyone, found a low branch, and looped the red ribbon around it to make a bow.

A shadow fell across the grass.

The elegant young lady was standing right beside me, her head tipped to one side like a squirrel assessing a nut. We stared at each other.

The young lady squeezed her handbag so tightly I thought she'd snap the straps. Her voice came out as a whisper.

"Ella?" Then stronger: "Ella-who-sews! It *is* you! Oh, Ella!" She dropped the handbag and flung her thin arms around me. "You're here! You came!"

Slowly my arms circled her. Slowly I breathed in the stupendous realization that this was actually, unbelievably, *her*. Not in a dream or just a whispered voice. Not even the shivering bag of bones I'd left coughing in a dirty bunk at Birchwood.

Trembling, I took her hands. I touched her face, her hair, her lips. Still I couldn't speak.

"Oh, Ella," she said, "have you any idea how happy I am to see you?"

I could only nod. Still speechless.

Rose chattered on, like the squirrel she was.

"I *told* Mama you're a survivor. I said, if anyone can get out of Birchwood in one piece, Ella can. You look so pale. . . . Are you all right? Do you need to sit down? *My* legs feel like jelly! Here, on the grass — oh no, you'll get your dress marked. It's an *amazing* dress. Is it your design? I *knew* it must be as soon as I saw you coming across the park. I couldn't believe it was really you, and then you took the ribbon out."

It fluttered above us, pinky-red among the white blossoms.

Relief, wonder, joy. All these feelings tumbled as tears out of my eyes and down my cheeks, spotting my pink dress.

"Are you all right? Speak to me, Ella. Say something!"

I took a deep breath, gave a little laugh and bowed.

"Will you . . . will you do me the honor of this dance?"

Rose looked baffled, then she too remembered our first day in the fitting room, when we'd polished the floor with mitts on our feet. Now, instead of her mismatched Birchwood shoes, she was neat in leather lace-ups.

"Well," she said with a smile. "Since you asked so nicely . . ."

We danced across the spring grass together, in the sweetest, happiest waltz ever. After a while we were laughing so much I got hiccups, and that made us both giggle even more.

"I thought you were *dead!*" I said suddenly, halting our waltz. "That everyone from the Hospital had gone up the . . . you know."

Rose clapped her hands to her mouth. "Oh, Ella, no! I'm so, so sorry. They cleared the Hospital and took us west — don't ask me why. Some crazy scheme to keep us from being liberated, I don't know. It was all so fast, there was no time to send a message or anything. I left you the ribbon so you'd have hope."

I squeezed her hand, tears pouring down my face. I couldn't bring myself to tell her I'd mourned her loss ever since I found that red ribbon.

* * *

"Rosalind?" As we approached, the cleaning lady at the dress shop shielded her eyes against the sun with her yellow mitts.

Rose and I burst out laughing. "That's not how you polish a floor!" we both said together.

"Mama, this is Ella!" cried Rose. "For real, and forever! Ella, this is my mother."

Rose's mama flung off her mitts and untied her apron. "*Ella,* come in! You are so very, very welcome. Perhaps now my daughter will stop telling me today is the day you'll arrive."

Later, after pink iced buns and lemonade, there was time for sharing news and questions. It was all so jumbled up. I heard how Rose had devoured the medicine I'd gotten for her, how that kept her alive to survive the journey out of Birchwood. "You'd be proud of me — I didn't share more than half of the vitamins," she boasted.

Rose had been transported in railway coal wagons to another prison camp . . . and another and another, each one more overcrowded and chaotic than the last, until the final camp was eventually liberated.

"With tanks and flags and everything," Rose said. "I tried to kiss the nearest soldier to thank him. He wrinkled his nose, poor soul — I was inches thick with filth — but he let me do it. Can you imagine how it felt to be given *real* clothes after those horrible stripes? Of course you can. I still can't get used to having a bra again. My straps keep falling down. But . . . enough about my adventures! What about you?"

"I haven't been kissing any soldiers!" I said, pretending to be offended.

Rose's mama declared there should be a statue to honor the farmer who'd saved me from death in the snow.

"I'll put your Flora in my next book!" she declared, waving her lemonade glass in the air as a salute. "The world needs more stories of *real* heroes. Especially ones who know one end of a cow from another. *I* certainly don't."

I laughed. "I never believed the stories Rose told, but it turns out you really are a writer, and Rose really is a countess, and you did actually live in a palace?"

Rose's mama looked a little offended. "But of course, my dear. Why would anyone think otherwise?"

Rose said, "Ella hasn't quite got the hang of stories, Mama. We'll have to work on her."

"Oh, don't talk about *work*," said her mama. "Have you seen the state of this place? We've been scrubbing and painting for an eternity to get it looking this good. What do you think?"

"Yes," cried Rose, springing to her feet. "What do you think, Ella? This front room will be the showroom eventually, with all the best gowns in the window display. In the meantime, I thought it would be nice to bring our tables in here, so people can watch us work as they go past. Mama's seen a second-hand sewing machine at the market. We'll all go together and buy it."

I smiled. "Another Betty?"

"Another Betty!"

Rose turned serious. "Have you heard anything about your grandparents?"

"Not yet. They weren't at home. I've been asking everywhere I go. I'll keep looking."

"And we'll help," Rose's mama said. "We'll scour the known world for news of your family. I still have some connections. If your grandparents can be found, we will find them — I promise."

Rose glanced at her mama and said nothing. I knew then that her papa had not been found. We weren't done with lists. We would scan lists every day, at train stations, synagogues, and refugee centers. We would scour the lists of survivors, even if Rose's father and my grandparents would never be found.

It was almost overwhelming, sitting in the empty shop, weaving a future from words, embroidered with dreams. The day dwindled and the street lamps were lit, their glow so much softer than the watchtower lamps at Birchwood.

Rose's mother watched me. "Your first commission is to make me a copy of that *divine* pink dress you're wearing. Where *did* you buy it?"

"I made it," I answered proudly, even though I was sharply conscious of all its faults. Every so often I imagined a prickle of mattress straw.

261

Rose smiled. "I told you she was good, Mama."

I said, "If we can get the fabric, I'll do a run of outfits for spring. Then everyone can have their own Liberation Dress — that's what I call this one." Something occurred to me, and I turned to Rose's mama. "If you don't mind my asking, how can you afford to rent this place? It's a lovely location, and in a really nice part of town."

"Oh we don't *rent*," she answered. "It's ours. Of course, it's nothing compared to the places we owned before the War. They were taken over by the military when my husband and I were arrested. The summer palace is gone for good, and the town houses and the cottage by the sea. This is the only one of the shop properties I have been able to claw back so far. And who cares, my darlings? You girls will sew and I'll scribble every hour night and day. And if we all wear outfits designed by you, Ella, all the fine ladies who see us will soon be clamoring to order some for themselves."

"Not forgetting the ring," said Rose.

"What ring?" I asked.

"The one you left for me at the Hospital . . ."

"*That* ring? I was sure Nurse Duck would've sold it straightaway and pocketed the cash. She really handed it over?"

"Of course. There wasn't time to barter it before the Hospital was cleared, so Duckie gave it to me, in case we got separated."

"Don't hold out any hope of getting a good price for the ring," I confessed. "It's a fake."

"Excuse me!" interrupted Rose's mama. "Are you calling that diamond a fake?"

"A really nice fake. It's just glass, I'm afraid."

Rose's mama held up one hand. "My dear, I've worn more diamonds than you've had hot dinners. I *think* I know the real thing when I see it."

Rose leaned close and whispered, "Plus we had it appraised at the jeweler's around the corner. It's real."

"And you don't mind using it, even though it was stolen?" I was still feeling a little guilty about using the money found in my Department Store coat.

Rose's mama frowned. "We'll never know who wore it first, or what's happened to them. If that ring can buy us a chance to live and work and love, so be it."

The upstairs room of the dress shop, with bare floorboards, bare bulb, and bare windows, was a veritable palace that evening. Rose and I shared one of the two mattresses, just as we had back at Birchwood. It was a million times more comfortable. We lay there, holding hands and grinning at each other.

"Tell me a dress to go with this place," Rose demanded, just like she used to.

"I can't. It would be a ball gown so dazzling it would blind you."

"I'd wear sunglasses."

There was a pause. I took a moment to appreciate exactly where I was and who I was with.

"I'm so sorry," I whispered suddenly.

Rose brushed a strand of new-growing hair from my face. "Sorry for what?"

"For . . . for being so horrible lots of the time. Bossy. Mean."

"I don't remember any of that!" she said with a laugh. "You were *strong*. You kept me going."

I shook my head. "No, it was *you* kept *me* going." Then, even more quietly than before—"How did you know I would come? How did you even know I'd survive?"

Equally quiet, Rose replied, "Because to think otherwise was unbearable."

Two days later I went up a stepladder to start painting the sign above our shop window. We'd argued and argued over what it should say. I wanted *Rose and Ella*. Rose wanted *Ella and Rose*. In the end we settled on a lovely scrolling design that said: THE RED RIBBON.

Afterword

The Red Ribbon is a story. Like Rose's tales, it is a mixture of truth and fiction. The truth is that Birchwood once existed for real. It was the vast labor and extermination camp complex called Auschwitz-Birkenau, in Poland.

Birkenau is a German word. I've translated it as "birchwood." During the Second World War, under the organization of the Nazi regime — and with the help and support of tens of thousands of ordinary people — millions suffered at Auschwitz-Birkenau, and at many hundreds of other camps and subcamps. This systematic degradation, displacement, and mass murder is now collectively known as the Holocaust. Victims were those considered "subhuman" by the Nazis. The death toll of those who died of starvation, disease, execution, and gassing with poison is horrifically high, estimated at 11 million, including 1.1 million children. At Auschwitz-Birkenau alone, well over a million people were murdered.

In the middle of this horror, the Auschwitz commandant's wife, Hedwig Höss (my Madam H.) truly did employ prisoners to work on her wardrobe. She began with seamstresses in a room of her house (a lovely villa built alongside the camp), then in 1943 she set up a camp workshop with twenty-three dressmakers, so that other officers' wives and female guards could wear the nicest fashions too. This workshop was first in a cellar, then in an abandoned factory building. It was called the Upper Tailoring Studio.

Mrs. Höss described her life in the house next door to Auschwitz as "paradise." She did indeed employ prisoners as household staff. She did also take one of her young sons with her to dress fittings, until a seamstress frightened him by looping a tape measure around his neck like a gallows noose when his mother wasn't looking.

After the war Hedwig Höss was captured with her children. Her husband Rudolf was convicted of war crimes and executed at Auschwitz. (One of the Höss daughters—not quite a teenager during the war—later worked for a Jewish fashion boutique in America, after a few years with the designer Balenciaga.)

For the sake of the story I've simplified the geography of the Auschwitz-Birkenau complex. I've tried to write clearly about the atrocities, selecting true incidents and scenarios, but my words don't come close to describing the full horror of the violence, the degradation, and the suffering.

The Red Ribbon is loosely set in 1944–1945. The summer

of 1944 saw staggering numbers of people transported from German-occupied territories and from Germany's allies all the way across Europe to Birkenau by train to be gassed. There was an uprising in October 1944 that was quickly suppressed. In January 1945, remaining prisoners were herded out of the camp complex on foot and dispersed to other killing zones in Europe. Their journeys were literally death marches. A few thousand remained in the camp, which was eventually liberated on January 27, 1945.

Descriptions in my novel of the Department Store (in reality known as "Canada," the land of plenty) are not an exaggeration. Mountains of shoes and other possessions are still on display in the Auschwitz museum. They are only a fraction of the plunder amassed. All were stolen from victims arriving at the Auschwitz complex. They survived the deliberate burnings at the end of the camp's existence. Even in the very last days, facing inevitable defeat, the Nazis wanted to hide evidence of their crimes.

Ella, Rose, Marta, and Carla might well have existed in Auschwitz-Birkenau, but they are all my own inventions. By coincidence, after writing the story I discovered that the real-life "boss" of the Upper Tailoring Studio was indeed named Marta, but survivors remember the real Marta as a kind and capable woman — so there is absolutely no association with my fictional character.

Each girl in *The Red Ribbon* highlights possible moral choices about surviving and thriving. They are choices we all make on some level, in humdrum day-to-day life as well as in extreme circumstances. In Auschwitz each person reacted as best they could. Sometimes their best was outstanding. Sometimes it was appalling. It can be dangerous to judge other people's behavior without knowing *why* they do what they do, and what pressures they were under. That said, I believe we all have to take responsibility for our actions, good and bad.

I have deliberately chosen not to dwell on specific countries, regimes, or religions in the story. This in no way devalues the reality that particular peoples were targeted for humiliation and genocide. The camps were designed to punish and annihilate specific groups of people. These included: enemies of the Nazi ideology; all Jewish people (regardless of nationality or faith practices); LGBTQ people; Romany communities; Jehovah's Witnesses; people with mental and physical disabilities; and others.

The majority of people murdered in Auschwitz were Jews. This must never be forgotten. Far from wanting to deny the historical truth of the Holocaust, I have spent many years reading wartime sources and survivor testimonies. I have long been haunted by the memoirs of women who actually labored in the workshops of the Auschwitz complex. I was even fortunate enough to talk with Eva Schloss, Anne Frank's stepsister, who worked in the clothing stores of "Canada." I was humbled and awestruck to look into Eva's eyes and to know that here was someone who'd experienced as *life* what the rest of us call *history*.

In *The Red Ribbon* my heartfelt aim has been to revisit a time in our past that clearly and categorically happened, but also to lift the stories out of historical specifics in order to show universal experiences. Hate crime, sadly, is not a thing of the past. It is preached as a policy, and also practiced in tiny everyday ways by people who ought to know better. You, me, anyone — when we divide the world into *us* and *them* we sow the seeds of hate. Hate blooms into violence. Violence kills us all, one way or another.

If we can see acts of kindness as acts of heroism, we can counter both the hatred and the violence.

I hope.